Cover photo by – Henry Gibbs

Max's Time Travelling

Adventure

(or 𝔚𝔢𝔫𝔡𝔩𝔢𝔰𝔟𝔦𝔯𝔦 Re-discovered)

To Isaac, Miles and Bennett,
I hope you enjoy this time travelling
adventure!
Best Wishes, Beverley Gibbs

By Beverley E Gibbs

First Published in 2018
ISBN – 13:978-1548931452

Dedication

This book is dedicated to my children Daniel, Mollie and Henry, who grew up during the 10 years it took me to write it, in the beautiful setting of Wandlebury, and to my husband Jon, who made that setting beautiful, magical and inspiring.

Acknowledgements:

Thank you so much to all my lovely friends and family, for their encouragement and support, which got me to the end, even if it did take 10 years.

Also to Bill for lending me his name, if not his character, and Wendy for her objectivity.

Finally, to Jose Reeve, who did the challenging job of reading, reviewing, and ultimately making me believe it was all worth the effort.

Preface

Shivering with cold, the soldier, so strong and solid, curled himself into a tight ball. The dim cellar displayed all the emotions he felt; confusion, bewilderment, but above all fear.

The soldier, in full Saxon military attire had separated from his battalion, on a reconnaissance mission, to seek a new and safe place to set up camp. The hill top setting seemed perfect, and as the light faded, he had pushed through some thick yew shrubbery, and found shelter to settle for the night. He'd been woken abruptly by the boy Albert, who had then threatened him with his own sword, and taken him prisoner.

His head throbbed, and the soldier involuntarily lifted his hand and touched the back of his neck. He knew Albert had pushed him hard, before locking him in the cold and damp cell.

The boy Albert tormented him, yet promised to help. Help to return him to his people. Albert had promised him food and shelter. This shelter was unlike any he had experienced. Cold, flat walls; rags on the floor and a utensil Albert called a bucket, sat in the corner. There was food, and water, both gratefully received. Yet there was something missing. His sword. Bronze, heavy and with an ornate handle inlaid with the reddest ruby.

From beyond the thick stone wall, came voices. There were two. They sounded young and excitable. Perhaps this was the help he had been promised?

So far from home, and embroiled in mystery, Oswulf the Younger sat tensely for a moment, straining his ears to listen. As the voices began to fade away, he leant back against the cold stone wall, deflated. He had been so sure help would be here soon. Hope was all he had, and he could not give it up. Not yet..

1
MOVING IN

Bleary eyed, Max anxiously pulled on his old grey dressing gown, shuffled into his worn plaid slippers, and stumbled towards the bedroom window. As he pulled back the dusty curtains, the early morning sun reflected a crisp white coating of frost.

'Wow,' Max exclaimed, 'that's wicked.'

His waking had disturbed other members of the household.

'Maxwell,' his dad called, from the far side of the cottage, 'it's only 6 o'clock, *and* it is Saturday. Please go back to bed.' But Max was too excited to go back to bed. He crept around his brother's bed and eased open the heavy wooden door. This was a big adventure to Max, and he wasn't planning to miss a single minute of this bright new day.

So this is Maxwell. An excited, quite clever, but not very brave 11-year-old boy. His dad George has just landed a fantastic new job as the Head Ranger looking after a huge woodland. Fantastic for his dad. Not so great for everyone else, or so it seemed at first. The new job was miles away, and everyone has had to move house. Everything had to be packed, and now unpacked. Everything from the pot in the garden with Grandpa's favourite rose (and nana's ashes) to Grandpa himself. All miles and miles away from all of their friends. It was especially hard for Max, who had to leave his best mate Danny. So you see, not so great.

But there's a good bit, and it's really good. The family; that is dad George Perry who you've already met, mum Martha, Max who you now know quite well, his little brother Archie aged just 7 and their baby sister Jessica. Not forgetting Grandpa Sid, the dog Boz, and cat Snudge. Together, as a family, they have moved into their new home. It is a large Victorian cottage, nestled in a magical woodland, between beech and hazel coppice. From every window, trees, trees and more trees, as far as they can see. A child's paradise.

Their new home provided more space and freedom than the family could ever have imagined. A large untidy garden to one side of the cottage, was overrun with nettles and bramble. Where once a productive vegetable patch had given pleasure and produce to the last family, now, what could only be described as a wilderness had taken its place. A large greenhouse sat behind the allotment area, looking redundant and sad. Nevertheless, Max's father George, was excited about his new dream job, and was sure his family would love it here.

By the time George was up and dressed on their first morning, Max had already managed to locate the packing case, containing the breakfast cereal, and when George came down to join him in the dreary kitchen, Max was secretly munching on handfuls of wheaty flakes. He attempted a sentence, but only succeeded in spraying George with a mouthful of half chewed cereal.

'Please Max, don't speak with your mouthful,' said George. He waited, while Max hurriedly swallowed.

'I just want to get out and explore dad. Can I go now?' Max's face was anxious; he was eager for adventure.

'I know how you feel Max, but it is still early, and we have lots of unpacking to do. Let's have a nice family breakfast when the others have surfaced, and then we can all go out for a walk together. I need to explore too, so try to be patient. Why don't you pop back upstairs and see if Archie is awake? But try not to wake mum, she's had a bad night with Jess. And please creep quietly past Grandpa's door too. The move has taken its toll on him.' George, always patient, and ever practical, sent his eldest son back upstairs, then proceeded to clear a space at the large kitchen table for breakfast.

Apart from Grandpa, the family were all up and cleared away after their breakfast, by 10.30. Archie had been the last to wake, and Max had almost resorted to pinching his little brother, when, fortunately for Archie a loud cry from Jess jolted him from his sleep. Max quickly changed tack and helped his brother into a warm tracksuit, then hurried him down to the breakfast table.

At last, they were all ready to get out and explore their new surroundings. While Martha tucked Jess into the large Silvercross pram, the boys swiftly pulled on their Wellington boots. It was a cold January morning, and as they opened the back door, a gust of wind blew a handful of crisp brown leaves in through the opening, and the boys hurried out. With Jess now safely strapped in, Martha manoeuvred the pram through the door. The ground was quite hard from an overnight snow shower, and with the temperature around freezing, gloves and hats were essential. George wore his regular work day uniform – khaki trousers, jacket and heavy walking boots. Archie was concerned.

'Are you going to work daddy?' he asked.

'No son,' George replied 'but I may meet some of my new work colleagues while we are out walking, and I want to give the right impression to them.' George took his young son by the hand 'when we get back, you can help me build a nice open fire, and we can all have hot chocolate to warm ourselves.' With that, he led Archie up the path and through the rickety gate, which took them out of their garden and into the park. The rest of the family followed.

Max felt a strange churning in his tummy. He usually felt this when he was excited, but this time he couldn't quite explain why he had this feeling. He supposed it was excitement. He instinctively knew one thing though. Things were going to be really good in their new home. The Perry family were all enthusiastic, as they set off to explore the vast expanse of wood and parkland, that was to become their new back garden.

2
EXPLORING THE PARK

The park is on a high point. There are 100 acres of dense, green, enchanting woodland, but also something else rather special. In the very centre of the park is an Iron Age ring ditch, where over 2000 years before them, Iron Age settlers had lived, and thrived. There were no trees in the ring back then, just a deep circular ditch. A perfect circle. 2000 years later, it is still there, with trees, shrubs, rabbits, deer and bats all sharing the same circular space. Lots of people visit the park every day. Ordinary people. Families with children, elderly people, nature lovers and bird watchers. This special place is called 'The Ring' because of it's perfectly circular shape and our family Perry are out to discover the magic of their new surroundings.

As the family strode into the park, the two boys stayed out in front leading the way. Their cottage was situated on the very outskirts of the site, and as they approached the circular ring ditch that gave the park its uniqueness, the boys ran ahead, and hurtled down the steep sides into the crisp remains of snow dusted autumn leaves below. George followed on behind, helping Martha with the pram. The ring ditch itself was no longer the deep defence structure that it would have been in Iron Age times. Many years of visitors to the site had shaped the character of the park. Horse chestnut, yew and lime trees over hung the ring, and dense shrubs lined the banks. Small clearings exposed pockets of yellow aconites and snowdrops. The family enjoyed a long walk around George's new emporium, really getting a feel for their new surroundings. As the boys darted in and out of the woodland, enjoying the freedom and fresh air, the family felt a new closeness and bonding that only this perfect setting could give.

Long after the Iron Age settlers, and Romans had made this their home, a Victorian Lord by the name of Greyford built a beautiful manor house in the very centre of the ring. Inside the boundary of the Iron Age ring ditch, he built a three-metre high, solid brick wall around his garden. This wall had 4 access points, barred by heavy wrought iron gates. After the death of his wife, he lived alone in 'Greyford Hall' as it was known, until his death in 1924. With no surviving family members to take over the estate, Lord Greyford chose to leave the land and buildings to charity. But years of neglect had resulted in Greyford Hall falling into disrepair, and the shell of this beautiful building now stood empty. The unusual one-handed clock on the tower showed a quarter past 11, and only the stable block and old servants quarters had been preserved. The brick wall was enveloped in ivy, and thousands of masonry bees had made tiny homes in the mortar and brickwork. Only two gates remained.

The family passed the ruins, and completed the circuit of the ring in 40 minutes, then headed back to the cottage, where the prospect of a roaring fire and warming hot chocolate awaited them. There would be plenty of days to come, when they would be able to explore the more extreme reaches of the park; the Roman Road bisecting the southern tip; the Victorian cottage garden and vegetable patch, within the walled garden; the wishing tree & the Celtic hill figure field. George, in particular, was looking forward to showing his family these treasures, hidden within the boundaries of their new home. But that was all for another day.

It was now January, the trees had shed their leaves, and the beautiful woodland, surrounding the fairytale cottage, enclosed and protected the young family. What magical secrets were held within such a forest? As the Perry family settled down to the second night in their new home, a soft hoot could be heard, the call of a tawny owl to his mate. The first proper plump flakes of snow began to fall, as a happy stillness descended, the house fell silent.

3
MEETING BILL

'Hello lad.' A friendly voice came straight from a thicket of smallish shrubs at the end of the woodland track. Like a strange ventriloquists act, there appeared to be nobody around. Max swung round, '..and what do they call you then?' There stood a friendly looking, fairly ordinary man, if not a little oddly dressed in cut off breeches and a loose untucked shirt. His face was gentle, kind even, and he had a very wide smile. Max was apprehensive. He had always been told not to talk to strangers, but somehow this man didn't seem like most strangers, it was as if he'd met him before, he just couldn't remember when. Max decided it would be impolite to ignore the man completely, but he unconsciously took a step back, before replying.

'My name is Maxwell Perry, but only mum and my Nanna Mary call me that, I'm Max to everyone else.' His voice was a little shaky, and he swallowed hard, then took a deep breath.

'Well, young Max, and I hope you won't mind me calling you Max? My name is Bill. I've lived here all my life, and I'm very pleased to meet you. If there is anything you want to know about the estate, I'm your man. Come and have a chat any time, I'm always around.' The old man paused. 'I can see you are anxious, so you get back off home now, and I hope we'll meet again. I'm in the cottage at the bottom of the track. Hope to see you again very soon. Goodbye for now Max, cheerio.' And with that the old man turned and walked back into the undergrowth. Max was rather taken aback with this old gentleman's friendliness.

'Yes sir, thank you,' Max called out, but by this time Bill was nowhere to be seen.

The woodland on either side of the path was dense and cold; Max felt a shiver run down his spine. It was the first time he had ventured out on his own, and already he had met a neighbour. He wasn't sure why it made him feel uneasy, the gentleman Bill was perfectly nice, yet something felt odd. As he made his way back up the track that led from the car park to the cottage, Max came to an opening by a big Yew Tree circle, which made a convenient cut through. His dad had told Max that these trees could live for hundreds, if not thousands of years, and Max made a mental note to ask his dad exactly how old their Yew trees were. At that point, as he pushed through a tangled web of ivy, Max carelessly caught his foot on a large root protruding from the ground, and he fell with a thud onto the firm undergrowth. No real damage was done, and, as Max pulled himself to his feet, something poking through the leaf litter caught his eye. A single sharp stone shaped to a point, about 1 centimetre visible and with a rugged uneven surface, was buried in the earth. Max brushed away some soil, and tugged at the stone. It was wedged in quite firmly. He dug around its edges until the object was released from its dirty resting place. Max tumbled backwards slightly, his hand tightly gripping the mysterious stone. Once he'd regained his composure, Max looked closely at his find. What a find it was. The whole object was about 6 centimetres in length, and 2 centimetres wide at its widest point.

'It's an arrowhead, I've found a Stone Age arrowhead,' Max whispered, to himself and his Yew tree audience. He was sure this was something special, and with the stone tightly clasped in his dirty fist, Max ran the short distance back to the cottage.

Once back home, Max raced through the back door, sending the family's small black cat, Snudge, flying for the safety of the large oak sideboard. The young boy could hardly contain his excitement, and raced up the stairs to share this find with his parents. Martha was changing Jess in the nursery, and briefly looked up when her son entered the room.

'Hello love, have you had a good morning?' His mother had already turned her attention back to the baby, and showed the usual amount of interest in what her son had been doing. Jess always needed his mother's full attention, so Max felt uneasy about telling her about his arrowhead.

'Yes mum, not bad. Where's dad?' Max decided he'd tell his father first, he was sure to get an excited reaction from him, and he could always tell mum later.

'Dad is in his office, but Max he is trying to work, so please don't disturb him.' Feeling deflated, Max turned and went back downstairs. In the lounge he found his younger brother Archie playing his latest Playstation game.

'Hey Arch, want to see what I found when I was out exploring?' Max hoped the treasure he had found would impress his little brother.

'Huh?' Archie kept his eyes firmly on the screen, 'tell me what it is.' Archie continued to furiously press the small black buttons on his control pad, whilst twisting his upper body from one side to the other.

'You need to stop playing that game and look at me' Max was getting a bit impatient. He now knew how his mum felt when she asked him to finish his game. It was impossible to explain why you can't just stop playing, without the game crashing, his character being captured by aliens, or something equally as disastrous. With this in mind, Max gave up on Archie, and turned out of the lounge, but as he passed the coat hooks in the hall, he caught sight of his grandfather's old flat cap. Why didn't he think of it earlier, Grandpa Sid? He would certainly take interest.

Max took his treasure through to the back room, which Grandpa called the parlour, and found his grandfather sitting by the fire, listening to the radio. He liked to spend quiet time alone in this room, but looked up and smiled when Max entered.

'Grandpa, I'm so pleased I've found you. I've got something very special to show you, *and* I've met one of our new neighbours, whose name is Bill and he lives in the round cottage at the bottom of the track.' Max was speaking at speed by this point, and his grandpa looked bewildered.

23

'Whoa, Max, slow down boy. It sounds like you've had an exciting morning, come and sit down, and tell me all about it.' Max had at last a captive audience. He launched into a detailed description of his morning; exploring the track down to the car park, meeting Bill, tripping over, and finally his special find. As he unwrapped the arrowhead, Grandpa Sid reached over to put on his glasses.

'Well Max, that really does look like something special. I feel honoured to be the first to see it. I suggest you put it away somewhere safe, then speak to your parents about it when they have a bit more time.' It was his grandpa's way of saying they probably wouldn't be that interested. Oh well, at least now he'd shown one member of his family, and an appreciative one at that.

Max wrapped the arrowhead in some discarded tissue paper and tucked it into his inside jacket pocket, and returned to his bedroom. He thought of his friend Danny, and wished he could just call him up. He was the only other person, who he knew would really appreciate the importance of his new possession. His mum had already said Danny could come to stay anytime, so Max decided now was the time to invite him. Danny would understand the importance of his news. 'I'll write to him' said Max to himself. He pulled out the new writing set his grandpa had given him for Christmas and sat down to write a long letter to his best friend. It would be great to see his old friend again. Once this was posted all he had to do was sit and wait.

4
DANNY COMES TO STAY

Max groaned as he pulled back his bedroom curtains. The clouds hung heavily in the dull grey sky. It was the first day of their school holiday, and Max's best friend Danny, was coming to stay. It was nearly three months since Max had last seen his best friend, but since that first letter, followed by several emails, it had been arranged that Danny could visit at Easter, and stay for 5 days with the Perry's. The 11.00 o'clock train from London's Liverpool Street Station, was due to arrive at Stapleton station at 12.18pm.

After his shower, Max took great care to choose a suitable outfit for the day. He was keen to impress Danny with his new lifestyle, and show him that living this far out into the country didn't mean they were completely out of touch with the rest of the world. At breakfast, George was noticeably absent. He'd gone out at dawn with his ferrets, and had yet to return. Max took his place by the window, and gazed out into the gloomy mist.

'When will dad be back?' Max asked his mum.

'I don't know exactly, Max, but I'm sure he won't be too much longer, after all he went out very early.' Martha's reply was quite curt. She had spent much of the night awake with a teething baby, and was now feeling tired.

'I hope he hasn't forgotten that Danny arrives today,' Max
filled his bowl with cereal and milk, 'only he promised I could go
with him to the station.'

Martha was busy picking up the squashed pieces of banana and rusk
that Jess had dropped on to the carpet, and as she returned to her
seat, she realised from the solemn look on his face, that her son was
genuinely anxious about his father returning on time.

'Don't worry Max; there is plenty of time before Danny's
train arrives. Dad needed to get out early, in order to be back in
plenty of time to collect Danny. After breakfast, why don't you go
up and sort out the bedroom ready for your guest, and before you
know it, it will be time to go and collect him?' Martha was always
keen for her children to help around the house, and the boys were
expected to keep their own rooms tidy. This suggestion did the trick,
and once Max had finished his breakfast, he ran up the uneven stairs,
two at a time, enthused by the prospect of seeing his old mate in a
few short hours.

The morning dragged, but Max did his best to tidy his room, clearing
a small area of floor, just large enough for an airbed. He carefully
emptied one drawer of his own clothes, for the use of his friend.
Lastly, Max checked the marble box for his most treasured
arrowhead, which lay safely where he'd left it. Everything was ready
for Danny's arrival, so Max grabbed his portable Gameboy and went
downstairs to wait.

The train was running 10 minutes late, but when it eventually pulled in, it was clear that Max and Danny were thrilled to see each other again. As they bundled into the back of George's old dirty four-wheel drive, together with one small holdall, they chattered non-stop about anything and everything, stopping only when they arrived back at the park. Max jumped out to open the large five bar gate for his dad, and then followed behind as the vehicle bumped up the rocky makeshift driveway. The boys went straight upstairs with Danny's bag, to the bedroom. Max then proudly showed his friend around the rest of the house, saving the cobweb-ridden cellar until last. Satisfied that all he had seen so far impressed Danny, Max took him back upstairs to change into something more casual before lunch, finding time to carefully slip the wrapped arrowhead into his belt bag.

After they had eaten, there was some discussion over what the boys could do that afternoon. Martha was in the house doing normal jobs, which meant Archie and Jess would be there too. Max didn't want to be stuck with entertaining his little brother, so suggested they should be allowed to go out and explore a little in the woods surrounding the cottage, but no further. Martha agreed to this, and the two older boys grinned at the prospect of spending the whole afternoon discovering the unknown.

In warm coats and boots, they ventured out. Although the day had brightened considerably, it was still cold for the time of year. This didn't stop the youngsters as they pushed into an area of undergrowth clearly visible from the house, which to them was a hideout only they knew about. Archie and Max had spent a significant amount of time over the previous weeks collecting small branches to build a small hideout. They had then transferred several plastic chairs from their old summer house, into this hidden retreat, in order to sit and gaze out, convinced they were invisible to the outside world. Max led the way. Once inside, Danny was really rather impressed.

'This is sort of like a bivouac built by the Scouts, except it should be waterproof, and you don't have a roof,' Danny continued, 'so, obviously yours isn't going to be waterproof!' Danny's dad was a Scout leader, and Danny had been camping with the Scouts as long as he could remember. He was still very impressed with his friend's creation, and ideas came flooding to him, of how they could improve it. It was now, however, Max's time to really impress him.

'Dan, I've got something really special to show you; *really* special,' he emphasised the fact that this was an important moment, and pulled his chair up closer to Danny. Max carefully pulled out the tissue wrapped parcel, pausing to ensure he had Danny's full attention. There was a real feeling of anticipation in the air, as the two boys looked at each other.

'Come on then, Max, open it up; let's see it.' Danny's voice was lightly mocking, yet as Max revealed the arrowhead, his jaw dropped slightly. There was a stunned silence. Danny knew exactly what it was, and was suitably impressed. 'That's a real arrowhead;

probably Stone Age by the look of it. Where did you get it?' Danny was by now leaning over his friend. 'Can I hold it?'

'You can, if you are really careful,' replied Max 'keep it wrapped in the tissue.' The arrowhead was passed to Danny, who took great care as he inspected the object up close. 'I'll take you to the place I found it, if you like. It isn't too far, I'm sure mum won't mind if we go a little way.'

As the boys departed their secret hideaway, the arrowhead carefully wrapped back up, and replaced in Max's belt bag, they chose to skirt around the back to avoid being seen from the house. The shrub layer was quite thick, and passing through it, their trousers gathered mossy green stains, and a dusty film covered their boots. The woodland became less dense, except for the giant rotten trunk of a fallen beech tree, which lay across their path. The boys helped each other over, before entering the Yew Tree Circle. Max turned around to get his bearings. Although he had returned to the exact spot where the item had been found, many times, he had previously always taken the footpath from his house, turning down the woodland track that led into the Yew Tree Circle from the other side.

'It's over here, Dan. I haven't seen anything similar, but I keep looking.' The boys brushed away the earth at the base of the largest yew.

'Let's go and explore some more Max.' Obvious that they weren't going to find anything this time, Danny was keen to get out into the main park, to see all the exciting things Max had described in his letters and emails.

'Mum doesn't let me go out into the park on my own. We can go out and do some exploring later when my dad is free, I think we should go back now.' Max didn't like disobeying his parents, but it was tempting with his friend here, not to bend the rules a little.

'Come on Max, they won't even know we've gone out – and you won't be on your own, you're with me! Be daring!' Danny had always been very persuasive, and Max really didn't want to lose face. A short while wouldn't hurt – would it? After a minute's pause, he decided.

'Ok Danny, let's take a chance, come on this way, I'll show you the ring ditch, but then we will *have* to go back to the hideout.' The boys turned out of the Yew Tree Circle heading for the orchard. Just before they reached the walled garden area within the ring, Danny turned left at the giant beech tree and ran down into the ring ditch. Max followed, and they kicked through the rotten remains of last year's fallen leaves as they ran carefree along the foot of the ditch. Impulsively, Max climbed the bank of the ditch, to a thickly hedged length of the ring. The ditch bank was particularly steep at this point, but Max had climbed it many times, and had perfected the knack of leaning forwards as he ran, whilst a quick sideways foot action allowed him to clamber crablike, ascending the bank with ease. Max called down to his friend,

'Come up here Dan, we might be able to squeeze through the hedge to the orchard.' Danny scrambled up the steep sides to join his friend. 'There's a small gap here, I think I can get through if I take off my coat.' The boys removed their jackets, then got down on their tummies, and crawled side-by-side commando-like through the small opening. As they emerged within the confines of the ring, a stunning and unbelievable sight beheld them.

5
SEEING ROMANS

'What is it, Max?' Danny whispered. 'It looks like Romans. You didn't tell me your dad had a Roman re-enactment group set up in the ring.'

'The reason for that Dan, is I didn't know anything about it. I'm as surprised as you are.' It really was an awesome sight for any 11-year-old, and these two were no exception. Stretched out in front of the boys, covering most of the lawn area, stood men in Roman costumes, several tents, old looking, brown and quite shabby. There were three or four horses tied up, and some small children sat together playing. They wore simple beige tunics, and funny looking hoods covered their small heads. One family group had a small fire in front of their tent, and appeared to be cooking on it. One of the men was dressed in full Roman soldier clothing. It was a truly contented scene, and Max neglected to notice that outside this exciting encampment, the setting had some major features missing.

'Let's go and ask dad if we can come back here and join in,' said Max. The boys wriggled back through the hedge, grabbed the jackets they had discarded earlier, then raced back to the cottage to relay what they had seen, to George. Max shouted as he entered the yard.

'Dad, dad,' Max pushed open the rickety gate, and it swung, screeching back on its rusty orange hinges, then ricocheted back into Danny, who was close on his heels.

'Hey, Max' Danny yelled '…remember me, ouch, my shin!' Danny couldn't avoid the gate, but followed his friend through with a limp as he clasped his sore leg.

'Sorry Dan, look there's my dad by the ferret's cage. Hey, dad..' George turned when he heard his son call.

'Hello boys, have you had fun out exploring?' George remembered his school days fondly. Many hours were spent building dens in the woods, or playing 'Cowboys and Indians' with friends. 'What have you been up to then?' George finished filling the water bottle, and attached it to the ferret's cage. 'You haven't been out long.' The boys looked at each other, and then Max spoke.

'Dad, the Roman camp, we were wondering if we could go and join in? We wouldn't interfere. We'd do as we are told. Please dad.'

Danny added 'Yes, please Mr Perry, it would be educational.' As the boys stepped back to wait for a response, they both took a deep breath. The excitement of what they had seen in the ring, combined with the race back to the cottage had left them both quite breathless. George, on the other hand, was looking puzzled.

'Sorry, Max; I don't quite understand what you are asking me. Slow down a bit, and go over it again.'

'The Roman camp, in the ring, Mr Perry. We sneaked through some bushes, and saw them all there, all dressed up, with horses and tents and everything.'

'Horses!' George's voice rose a pitch, '..and tents.'

'Yes dad. We wondered how long it is going to be there for, as you hadn't mentioned it before.'

'I don't know anything about an event in the ring this weekend, unless I haven't been told about it. No one should be erecting tents or taking horses in to the ring. I can get into trouble with English Heritage, within the ring area is designated as an ancient monument.' George appeared to be getting quite anxious as he spoke. He strode past the boys and into the kitchen. Max and Danny followed.

'I need to go over and see what is going on, you boys can come with me. I'm just going to change my trousers, I suggest you two do the same, you certainly look like you've been scrabbling about on the banks of the ring ditch, your knees are filthy. I'll meet you back down here in five minutes,' and with that George strode out of the kitchen and up the stairs. Max and Danny followed. Once in the bedroom, Max carefully emptied his trouser pockets onto the dressing table, taking care to place his special stone from his belt bag on to the tray where all his precious things lived. It was the oldest object he owned, and he didn't want to risk losing it. The boys both changed into something clean, and returned to the kitchen where George was waiting.

George walked briskly, and the boys had to jog to keep up with him. When they reached the large beech, which was adjacent to the western entrance to the ring, George turned right into the orchard. They passed through the wrought iron kissing gate, set in the

Victorian ivy-clad brick wall and stood in the centre of the ring. It was empty. No Romans. No tents. No horses. The boys were aghast, and it was several seconds before Max could take it in. George was not very happy.

'Good one boys. You had me fooled. Do you think I have time to mess about with schoolboy pranks? It isn't funny, and I really have got things I should be doing this afternoon.' Max and Danny couldn't understand what had happened. How had the ring been cleared of all those Romans, and all their accoutrements in such a short time? They weren't even packing up when Max and Danny had watched them earlier.

'But dad, I don't understand. They were here. Fires burning, and children all dressed up, we weren't making it up, we really weren't.' Max felt totally bewildered. He knew what he had seen earlier, they both did. His father had by this time turned, and started to walk over to the office building, which was housed in one of the converted stable blocks. Max turned to Danny.

'It's no good Dan, he doesn't believe us.' Max felt completely frustrated with the situation. 'Let's go back now, I'm feeling a bit chilly.' The boys' mood had slumped, and they slowly took the same path back home, in silence. Neither boy knew what to say. Max went over and over what had happened, in his head. Danny was doing the same. There didn't seem to be the words to express the unbelievable. Something had been there, as large as life, as they say, and then it had gone. Like magic, or some kind of miracle.

When the boys arrived back home they sloped up to Max's bedroom, with their tails between their legs. Max carelessly switched on his Playstation, and the boys sat down to play in silence. After a short while it was Danny who broke the silence.

'We didn't imagine it Max. We both saw them, we need to go back. Why don't we go when your parents are asleep? It might be something to do with the way we entered the ring.' Max, being generally cautious wasn't sure about this idea.

'I s'pose, but I'm not sure about going at night.'

'Oh Max, it will be an adventure. Come on, what can happen?' Danny could be quite persuasive, and Max was very puzzled about the day's events.

'Ok, yes, let's go tonight. We will have to plan it properly, I'll put my alarm on to wake us, and we will have to be really quiet,' Max felt a flutter of excitement inside; this would be a real adventure. At that point he glanced up and caught sight of the discarded arrowhead lying on the dressing table. He decided he'd take it with him when they went back later – like a kind of 'Good Luck' charm.

The boys whiled away the rest of the evening, every glance across the dinner table held a guilty secret. The time really dragged by, and after several games of rummy with Grandpa, the boys said their goodnights, and retired safely to Max's bedroom – earlier than usual. It had been difficult to keep quiet about their plan, but they'd agreed it was best just to say nothing that evening, and kept conversation down to the barest minimum. George and Martha assumed the day's events had left them feeling guilty and sombre. Nothing more had been said, but it wasn't in George's nature to bear a grudge, and boys could be so imaginative. He put it down to the excitement the boys felt, being united after so long. It would all be forgotten by the morning, and George thought it best to leave the boys alone for now.

6
RETURNING TO CAMP

The boys' alarm went off at 4.50am, just as planned, but Danny was only slightly roused from a very deep slumber. Max, on the other hand, leapt from his bed, and loudly whispered to Danny that it was time. A bright full moon shone through the bedroom window, and a criss-cross shadow was thrown onto the simple duvet cover. It was a beautiful clear night, the stars clearly visible, patterned the night sky. The young adventurers couldn't have wished for better conditions. Max dressed quickly, and after several minutes of cajoling, Danny was forced out of his sleep and into his clothes.

As Max carefully opened the door to his bedroom, and stepped onto the landing, he took care to hold on tightly to his trainers. Any abrupt sound could wake his parents, or worse still Jess. Danny followed close behind in stockinged feet, carefully closing the door behind him. He tugged at Max's shirt,

'What now?' Max whispered,

'Have you got your special stone arrowhead?' Danny's whisper was croaky.

'Yes' replied Max, 'now don't speak again until we are outside, just follow me.'

The two boys tried hard to creep down the old staircase, but it creaked on almost every step. There was a stirring from George's bedroom, which caused the boys to freeze.

'Let's make a dash for it.' Danny's whisper was strained.

'Okay, but mind the dog, he doesn't bark but don't fuss him or he'll whimper.'

They jumped the last few steps onto the cold stone tiles, which covered the floor of the large open hall. It was still dark, but as they pulled on their shoes and fleece jackets, a warm rush of excitement and adrenaline flowed through their bodies. The back door eased open without a sound, and Max led the way around the rear of the cottage. A cloud had temporarily dimmed the moonlight, but the boys were still able to pick their way down the path. The hoot of a distant owl reminded them that they should really still be fast asleep. Turning left out of the gate, Max, followed by Danny, briskly half walked, half ran the short distance to the Yew Tree Circle. As they retraced their steps from the previous afternoon, their pace quickened until they reached the exact spot in the ring ditch that they had entered the ring previously. Max spoke first;

'I think it is important we go in at the same point, don't you?' Trying to sound confident, Max was actually now feeling a little nervous. What were they expecting to find? Was it all a bit silly to think things may be any different from yesterday's events with his father? He began to seriously doubt himself now; after all, he had grown out of believing in magic, tooth fairies and all that Easter bunny nonsense. As all these thoughts tangled themselves in his head, it was Danny who moved first.

'Race you to the top, then let's wriggle under with our jackets on – it's too cold to strip off – go!' And with that Danny skipped sideways up the steep bank, just as he had seen his friend do the day before, reaching the top in seconds. Max didn't need telling twice, and all thoughts and doubts he'd been having vanished. He followed his friend immediately. Once at the top the boys looked at each other again. The moon had now brightened, and without any further words, the boys dropped to the ground and wriggled through the hedge opening.

As Max and Danny emerged on the other side of the hedge, taking them within the ancient Iron Age ring, beyond the ditch, the banks of which they had climbed so expertly, the sight left the boys with a huge sense of satisfaction. There were only two tents, less than previously, two sleeping Roman soldiers lying on a piece of sacking, and an open fire just in front of them. There was a small goat tethered to a tree behind one of the tents, and a small three-legged stool was placed at its entrance. The door to one tent was wide open, and the second was loosely tied shut. Danny got to his feet.

'Hey, what do you think you are doing?' Max's voice was filled with panic, 'I don't think that's a good idea; get back down here, they might see you.'

'Come on Max, we've got to sort out the mystery, it's what we came back for.' As Danny moved towards the camp, Max called him back.

'Well, wait one minute, I've got a strange warm feeling in my pocket.' Danny, ever the joker, responded instantly,

'Oh Max, so scared you've wet yourself, have you?' He laughed out loud. At this point, one of the Roman soldiers stirred and grunted in his sleep. An empty ale tankard lay by his side; it was unlikely that he would wake for several hours. Max was cross at his friend for disturbing the man, and for generally not following their plan.

'Don't be stupid Dan,' Max pulled himself up, and felt in his pocket, 'it's my arrowhead, it feels warm, here feel it.' Max pulled the object out of his pocket. It wasn't burning hot, but it was emitting a gentle heat. As he handed it to Danny, it appeared to glow.

'It's like a sign; something weird is happening, I think we should go into the camp to see if anyone is awake, then we can find out where they have all come from.'

'Right Max, how about we walk around the outside,' but at that point, a look of panic shot across Max's face. 'Max, are you ok?'

'I..' Max hesitated, 'I have just realised that we are in the orchard.'

'Duh, yes we already knew that.' Danny was getting impatient now. But Max still looked deadly serious, brushing off his friend's sarcasm.

'So where have all the fruit trees gone, and where is the old wall? These people are camping where the orchard should be, and the Victorian cottage garden – that's missing too. Dan, I don't like this, it's spooking me.' Max felt more uneasy, the more he thought

41

about it. None of this made any sense. Things were missing. All they'd done was crawl into the orchard under the hedge, instead of using the path and gate. Now the orchard seemed to have disappeared. The gate, the wall and even the derelict old house were nowhere to be seen.

'Dan, let's go back, I've changed my mind,' but as he said this Danny's determination to investigate further was made evident.

'No Max! I'm going through the middle to see if I can find someone awake,' and with that Danny stepped out into the area within the ring ditch, where the Roman men were sleeping peacefully. Max, with a tightness in his chest, and clenched fists, not brave enough to return by himself, followed his friend into the ring.

The boys had only covered a few metres when they heard a voice, clearly directed at them, and appearing to come from the back of the nearest tent.

'I see you have discovered the key?' The voice had a familiar tone to Max, but he couldn't quite place it, 'young Max, I wondered how long it would be before you made this discovery, and I must say you have been remarkably quick – and you have brought a friend.' As the boys stood waiting to meet the owner of this voice, a small friendly person emerged from behind the tent.

'Bill!' Max exclaimed, a feeling of relief flooding through him. 'We have been wondering what is going on, what has happened to the orchard? It is all really puzzling.'

'What is equally puzzling,' Bill replied, 'is why you two boys are up at 5 in the morning, but then, as you are the new keeper of the key, it is perhaps your will now to travel.'

It was Max's turn now to be puzzled.

'I'm sorry Bill, I don't understand what you mean. My friend Danny and I have just come to explore. It is easier to do it when mum and dad are in bed.' Bill smiled. The boys clearly didn't realise the journey they had made, and what an incredible discovery that arrowhead really was. It was time to explain things.

'Come and walk with me, boys, and I will explain, but be prepared to hear some surprising facts.'

The boys approached Bill, and walked with him, as he took the path steering clear of the tents. As they passed the open tent, they peered in. Two small children were sleeping just inside the opening. They couldn't see very clearly, and didn't like to stare too obviously, but the children appeared to be wearing white cotton hoods.

'Now Max,' Bill spoke slowly, and the boys waited with anticipation. 'You hold the key that is transporting you to this point in time. The year is 142ad, and Wandle Park, or rather Wendlesbiri as it was known, is not the country park you now know it to be. The two Roman families we have just passed, sleeping in their tents, are passing through, on their way to London. They will probably stay here for a few days, while they gather some food for their journey. It is a regular overnight camping spot for families in Roman Britain. You know that there is a Roman road adjacent to the country park don't you?' Both boys nodded. 'This has been used by people in this country travelling to London from the coast for two hundred years. You two are privileged to be witnessing their ancient way of life. Come, follow me, I will show you something you will recognise – this hasn't changed in two thousand years.'

The boys glanced at each other, then followed Bill, unable to comprehend what they were being told. Bill crossed the grassy area Max knew to be the orchard, and dropped down into a barren sloped ditch type area.

'Do you know where you are now, boys?' Bill had a wry smile on his face. Danny and Max were, by now, quite disorientated. Max spoke first, 'I don't mean to be rude Bill, but I think we should be getting back now, and I really don't know where we are.' His voice was slightly shaky, and his face showed more than a little concern.

'Don't worry lad, I'll get you back before anyone knows you've been out of your beds, I just have a little bit more to explain.'

Bill proceeded to show the two 21st century boys, that they were standing in an area they now know to be the edge of the Iron Age ring ditch. Beyond the ditch was a further ditch, deeper than the first, and the view beyond stretched out over the great city. They had somehow been transported back from the year 2018ad to the year 142ad.

Danny still had many questions to ask Bill, and was eager to get his head around what had actually happened to them.

'Bill, you haven't said why we are here, what is this 'key' you mentioned?' He waited with bated breath for Bill to respond.

'I'm glad you were listening Danny, as the key is in Max's pocket. Max put his hand back into his pocket and pulled out the stone arrowhead. It was still warm, and Max reluctantly placed it in Bill's outstretched hand. 'This key has been missing for over 1000 years. The last person to have it, travelled with it as you have done, but it was lost around the year 940ad. Your yew trees have kept it safe for all those years. It will allow you to travel between times into the ring, whenever you have it in your possession, but never lose it whilst on your travels, or you may not be able to return home.'

The boys stood in stunned silence. It would take some time to take this all in. They had simply expected to come out at night for a little adventure; little imagining it would spiral into something as serious as time travelling. Bill hadn't finished,

'I should mention to you Max, that you have this key for a reason, you could call it a mission. At some point in time a Saxon soldier became caught up with the holder of the key, and was transported forwards in time, where he has stayed. Along the way he lost, or had stolen, a vital precious item. You need to help him return. You must find this item, and the soldier, then, as custodian of the key, you are the only one who can help him get back to his own time zone, it is your duty.' At this news, Danny beamed, but Max looked quite horrified. He had only really been brave enough to come this far because Danny had pushed the idea, now he would be forced to carry on.

'Bill, how come you are here?' Max asked.

'Ah, Max, I wondered when you would ask me that. I have been able to time travel since I was a boy. I have seen all the changes here to this wonderful park, but I don't possess the key, and so I haven't been able to help this poor fellow from Anglo-Saxon Britain – although I have communicated with him at length. It is getting late now, and I need to return home,' Bill turned towards the boys, 'I suggest you two do the same. Don't lose that arrowhead now, and make sure you leave the ring at the exact spot that you entered.'

The boys instinctively looked back across the ring, past the two remaining tents to locate that spot. When they turned back, Bill had gone. He had made no sound, just simply vanished.

'Come on Dan, let's go home, I'm not sure quite how to describe what we've just experienced, but I know we had better be getting back home. If my mum and dad catch us we will be grounded, and certainly no more adventures these holidays.'

The boys were careful to locate the exact spot in the hedge, where they had entered the ring. With Bill's instruction still clear in their minds, the mixed holly and blackthorn bushes looked vaguely dishevelled at a certain place. Max turned to Danny,

'It's here, I'm sure. Let's get through as quickly as we can. Get down low like we did when we came in.' Both boys, first Max then Danny made a smooth exit, descending the bank on the other side with ease. An eerie silence hung in the air, and as the boys picked their way through the woodland, with the still bright moonlight to aid their passage, neither child spoke a word. Danny wrapped his open jacket around himself with a hug. Max did the same, and as the feeling of cold, suddenly enveloped him, he gave a shudder. During their time with the Romans, neither boy had felt the cold, yet now it was quite tangible.

As they made their way back home in silence, questions were filling their young heads. The adventure had been a complete success and had answered the many uncertainties of the previous day that had been puzzling them. However, this new experience had left them with the taste for adventure and so many more questions now needed answers. As they picked their way back through the undergrowth, crossing the Yew Tree Circle to the cottage beyond, they were relieved to see the building was still in complete darkness. The small front gate had been left wedged open, and as they passed through Max glanced back at his friend and grinned. Danny smiled back. It was fair to say, that Max had been pushed to his absolute limit of courageousness, but now was feeling quite pleased with himself. As they crept back in through the back door, the front room clock chimed, one, two, three, four, five. Five chimes.

'Max,' whispered Danny as they climbed the stairs, 'did you count the clock chimes?'

'Yes Dan,' replied Max with a surprised tone to his voice, 'only five. And yet we left the house at just before five, and we have been out for much longer than five minutes. It seems as if there are even more secrets to this mystery than we thought.'

The boys carefully removed their coats, and after quietly undressing they slipped back into their pyjamas. It was a matter of minutes before exhaustion finally caught up with the boys and they drifted into a dreamful sleep.

~

Danny's stay at the Perry's soon came to an end. The days following the night time adventure had been boring in comparison, yet neither Max nor Danny had felt the need to test the magic key again. The friends agreed to meet up in the summer, when the weather would be warmer, and evenings longer. Their adventure was never discussed, but as Danny waved goodbye to his time travelling companion, Max gave him a knowing wink.

7
TALKING TO GRANDPA SID

As the long summer break drew ever closer, Max and Danny spent more and more time locked into a cyberspace union, exchanging their plans and thoughts via text message and email. The ideas grown over the previous two months had developed and intensified the boys' desire to go back to the ring with the special key. Their secret mission to rescue the unknown soldier seemed unreal. Until they could get their heads together and finalise plans face to face, they resigned themselves to an electronic communication and the odd telephone call, when one or other of the boys had any credit on his mobile.

The school term ended, on a beautiful warm, clear, July day. A completely cloudless sky paved the way for six weeks of sun. The Perry family had a short holiday planned for the end of the summer break, but the first three weeks of the summer holiday would be their own to spend at home with friends and family. It would be a busy time for George, with many family events planned in the park. Max would probably keep out of his way.

Grandpa Sid, however, was always there. Someone to chat to when Max was happy or comfort him when he felt sad. He knew so much. Useful, interesting things, and Max learnt lots from his grandpa. Mainly, Grandpa was a person Max looked up to and respected. He loved his grandpa, and wanted to include him in his secret, if only he would listen.

This bright July morning, Grandpa Sid was up early, out watering his vegetable garden. The courgettes were his favourites. Huge bushy plants which he had grown from tiny seeds. He hoped they would win him a prize at the village show. Grandpa's belief was that early morning watering was the secret to giant vegetables! In this new garden, there was lots of work to do, to make it as productive as the previous one, and Max knew that was where he would find his grandpa, that morning.

'Good morning Grandpa,' the old man looked up, startled. It was unusual for either of his grandsons to be up this early, especially in the holidays. He put down his old tin watering can and gently eased himself up to face Max, rubbing the base of his spine as he did so.

'Good morning Max, couldn't you sleep?' Max shook his head. 'Well I could do with a break now, so shall we go inside for a nice cup of tea?' Max smiled and turned to lead the way back into the house. Inside Grandpa's parlour, a fire was gently glowing in the fireplace. He kept a small fire burning all year, whatever the weather. After filling the teapot with freshly boiled water from the kettle, they settled down on the old worn sofa together.

'Grandpa, did I tell you about the adventure I had with Danny at Easter?' Max hesitantly addressed his grandfather, looking as he did so, straight into the embers of the glowing fire. Sid looked across at Max.

'You showed me your special arrowhead, but I don't remember you talking about a particular adventure. But my memory isn't what it was. Tell me now, if you like. I expect you are hoping for more fun when Danny arrives?'

Sid was mentally very alert, even if his bones were a bit creaky! Max knew he hadn't spoken about the time travelling, and had just been testing the water with this question. So far, so good. He decided to continue.

'I have been thinking about what Danny and I can do when he arrives tomorrow.' Max looked across to his grandpa. 'You remember my Stone Age arrowhead, but I didn't tell you it was actually a magic arrowhead, did I?' Max looked up, and saw a smile creep across his grandpa's face. A sinking feeling, and anxiety to make his grandpa believe him, caused him to babble on. '*Really*, Grandpa, please believe me, it helped us to time travel back to the Roman year of 147AD.' Sid was still smiling.

'Go on son. Explain to me how it did that then.' Sid poured out the tea, and leant back on the sofa with his mug warming his hands. Max released a huge sigh and began a full and detailed explanation of the episode with the Romans, and meeting Bill. As he did so, his grandpa nodded.

'So Max, let me get this clear. The circular Iron Age ring ditch, that currently makes up this lovely park that your dad manages, is actually a portal to travel in time?'

'Yes! Exactly that,' said Max excitedly.

'And when you pass through the hedge, which lines the circumference of the ditch, with your arrowhead in your pocket, you travel back to 147AD. Is that it?' Sid looked at Max.

'Yes. Well, yes and no. We did go to the Roman time, but that doesn't mean that is the *only* year we can travel to.'

'Ah, so perhaps these holidays, you could travel to another point in time? Victorian perhaps?' The question in the old man's voice, wasn't mocking, but Max was unsure whether his grandpa really did believe him. It seemed like he did. He hoped desperately that he did.

'Well Max, you did have some fun at Easter. But be very careful where magic is concerned.'

'But you do believe it Grandpa, don't you?' Max willed his grandpa to say yes. After a short pause, his grandpa gave a tactical response.

'I know how imaginative you can be when you and Danny get together. I believe you will have a fun time exploring the woods this summer,' he shuffled his cushions about, then sunk himself into them, 'can you put the radio on for me when you get up. Thanks lad.' It was Max's cue to leave, but not without a last quip. 'And you mind your manners, if you go meeting Queen Victoria on your next time travelling adventure.' He winked and smiled kindly.

Max did as he was told.

'See you later Grandpa,' he said as he left the parlour and went back up to his room. He puzzled over the conversation. He was encouraged by his grandpa's interest, but also felt a little disappointed. Perhaps he thought the time travelling story had been just that; a story. Well, Danny was arriving tomorrow, and then they would prove the magic was real. A new adventure was just hours away, he could feel it already, and he could not wait!

8
1861

'Charlie, Charlie, wake up!' A loud rapping on the door slowly brought Charlie to his senses. As he struggled to open his tired, sleep filled eyes, Charlie Clark heard his name being called in a loud whisper from behind the bedroom door, which led out onto the small attic landing. He recognised the voice at once, and realised that it meant, yet again, he had overslept. The voice belonged to Molly, the laundry maid and Charlie's best friend. If the truth were known, his only friend, and just like a big sister. This wasn't the first time she had saved his skin.

Charlie clambered off his hard mattress and pulled on a pair of torn brown britches, dragging the braces over his shoulders. His night shirt doubled as a day shirt as Charlie only had two of these; the other hung on the back of his door, crumpled but clean. Thanks to Molly it had been smuggled into the laundry two days previously, and was now almost dry. Apart from a small wooden chair to place his clothes on at night, and the mattress with a tired green blanket covering it, all he had in his room was a low stool to hold his grey tin candlestick holder.

Charlie opened his door and Molly rushed in. She lit the candle, which instantly brought a small glow to the dim space. Molly pulled back the single curtain that covered the solitary window. The sky was still black, but no stars could be seen. It was 4.50 am and past the time that Charlie should have started work.

'I can't keep doing this for you Charlie,' Molly whispered anxiously. 'You are going to be turned out one of these days, if ever Lord Greyford gets to hear about it.'

Charlie Clark was 11 years old, with jet black hair and a cheeky smile. He'd been taken on as chimney sweep and fire boy some 6 months earlier by the butler of the Manor House. It had been a wonderful day for Charlie. He had spent the previous 5 years in the workhouse. His life before the workhouse had been happy until tragedy had struck. First his kindly but strict father, was struck down and killed by an outbreak of smallpox. It was a sad time for his mother, Hannah, as she grieved for the loss of her husband, whilst desperately trying to comfort her son, and keep the home going. Within three weeks of his father's funeral, the money was all gone. Even selling everything they possessed, bar the clothes on their backs still wasn't enough for the small family to keep the family home, and their unsympathetic landlord turned Charlie and his mother out. Their only option was the workhouse, where they would be separated, and given food and shelter, in return for work. His gentle mother was distraught at the prospect of being separated from her only son, but with no other option available to them, they had entered the local workhouse together one windy Thursday evening, Hannah carrying a small leather bag containing their few possessions.

The small frightened boy, and his anxious mother spent their first night together, before the six-year-old Charlie was taken to the boys wing. Within days it was clear his mother had also contracted smallpox and was isolated in a medical room. Charlie was permitted to visit her once, before he was informed that she too had passed away. His sweet caring mother; gone. Charlie had felt his life was over, with no one left to care for him, it felt like life was not worth living. He spent the following weeks and months in a daze, following the other boys in lessons, chores and prayer. His life would follow this same monotony for the next 5 years. His time there was not a happy one. All the children had jobs to do, and were beaten severely by the elderly matron if they didn't carry out the duties to her satisfaction. The food was tasteless; thin gruel and a small amount of bread and cheese. Sleep was restless, the iron beds did not allow room to move about, and the noise of creaking metal and springs disturbed the heaviest sleeper. As time went on, Charlie tried hard to keep out of trouble. He enjoyed the school work more than his chores, and managed to avoid excessive unnecessary punishment from the workhouse Guardians.

When Charlie was 11, he was selected by a regular visitor to the workhouse, as a suitable boy to work on an estate in the neighbouring county called Wandle Park. When the day came to leave, Charlie had packed up his few belongings, and without even time to say farewell to the few friends he had made during his time at the workhouse, travelled in the carriage sent by the man, to the Manor House, called Greyford Hall.

Charlie's journey to his new home had been a long and very tiring one. The carriage was draughty, with the ruts on the road making it a very bumpy ride. The occupants of the carriage were visibly moved from their seats as they progressed on their way, using every ounce of strength to remain seated, they strained to avoid accidental collision with one another. Charlie tried to doze, but the uneven track persisted in jolting him awake at every rut and fissure. After what seemed to Charlie like an eternity, the carriage came to a sudden halt which brought him back to consciousness. He had sat listening to the voices outside, nervous and excited, completely unaware of what awaited him in this next phase of his, so far short, but eventful life.

'Charlie Clark,' a low loud gruff voice had called his name. Charlie moved out of his seat where he had been positioned to the right of an elderly gentleman in a long black coat and top hat. To Charlie's right had sat a small mousy lady who spent the whole journey with her head bowed and her hands clasped together, as if she were in prayer. Neither of his travelling companions had spoken. He'd moved to the carriage doorway and peered out. As he did so the door opened. A bright moon lit up an otherwise dark evening, illuminating a face he recognised. It was the man who had selected Charlie when he visited the workhouse.

'Come Charlie, quickly boy,' the voice softened, 'that's it, mind your step.' Charlie took the man's hand as he helped him down from the carriage. Charlie's small bag was thrown down from the luggage rack, and within minutes the carriage had disappeared into the darkness.

'Now lad' the man picked up the bag, 'we have a long walk across the field here, are you feeling strong?' Charlie wasn't sure whether the question required an answer, but he nodded anyway. The truth was that Charlie felt very tired. The tense, uncomfortable journey, together with a complete lack of restful sleep had started to take its toll on the young boy. The man walked briskly off in the direction of a densely wooded area, fortunately their passage was lit by the moonlight, and after a short while he introduced himself to Charlie.

'I suppose you would like to know a little bit about your new position at Wandle Park? I'm Reynolds – the butler to Lord and Lady Greyford. You will take your instructions from me.' At this point Reynolds' voice altered slightly in its tone, as if he had changed from friend to superior. He continued. 'There are many rules of the house, but it will take you time to take all this in. Above all, you must remember to keep below stairs at all times in order to avoid being seen by the family. Lady Greyford, in particular, takes great offence at the sight of servants above stairs. All your work must be done before they rise in the morning, or after they have vacated the rooms you will be working in.' His explanations had been clear, and the boy tried hard to visualise the set up that had been explained to him. A large house; it had to be large if a 'Lord and Lady' lived there, plus servants and lots of rooms, some below stairs. This was to be a completely new experience for the young boy. As they continued the stroll to his new home, Reynolds explained the role that Charlie would play as the fire boy. Apparently, the previous boy had died of consumption, but by all accounts, had always been quite sickly. Charlie would be working alongside a girl called Molly and she was a laundry maid.

The pair walked for a long while through the woods, their idle chatter diminished, until it was replaced by a determined silence, which engulfed more than just their space. On reaching the Manor House, as it was known, Charlie was taken around the back and in through a small wooden back door, which opened on to a staircase, that descended to another larger door. This was the servant's entrance. Charlie was told to use either this or the kitchen to go in and out of the house. Behind the door, a corridor stretched out before them, lit by a single candle at each end. He followed Reynolds through another door and into a large warm kitchen.

At first it had been like having a family again for Charlie. He had his own room, with a few possessions. Meal time was spent with the other servants in the big kitchen. Most had been kind to him, but none were as kind as Molly. At 16, Molly was in charge of beds and laundry, but kept a special eye on Charlie. She taught him how to black the grates and lay the fires in every room of the big house.

Twenty-two fire places in total. Charlie had to make sure the main living room, dining room and drawing room were laid, stoked and roaring by the time the family came down to breakfast. As it took a good hour to warm the large high-ceilinged rooms, Charlie had to be up and working on the first room by 4.30am at the latest. In addition to this work, he had to make sure all fires were extinguished, safe and clean before he could retire each evening. He had a short one-hour break in the middle of each day, but apart from this was on the go from early morning until late at night. Charlie's dream was to learn to read, and perhaps even to write, but this seemed an unrealistic dream when he could hardly keep his eyes open during his break, let alone do anything more. His job was tiring, and he only had one day off each month. After six months at the Manor House, Charlie was feeling as unhappy as he had felt at the workhouse.

'Come on Charlie Clark, get yourself moving, those fires will not lay themselves you know.' Molly's voice trailed off as she trotted down the narrow wooden staircase that led to the main house. Charlie was jolted from his reminiscing, and jumped to his feet.

'Only two more days to get through,' thought Charlie 'and then it will be my day off. I can sleep all day if I wish.' As he left his small room, Charlie slung a waistcoat over his shoulder and planted an old brown tweed cap firmly on his head, before hastily following Molly down the stairs.

9
MAX AND ARCHIE

After the chat with his grandpa, Max felt more determined than ever to carry out the mission they had been set, to rescue a Saxon soldier. He went through the plans he had made with Danny for the summer holidays, and made sure everything was ready in his room for Danny's arrival. He also decided it was time to let his younger brother Archie in on his secret. During the approach to the long summer break, Max had spent quite a lot of time with Archie. They built themselves a spectacular new shelter in the wooded area between the house and the Yew Tree Circle. Hidden in the woods, further from the old shelter but still quite close to home, so that mum wouldn't worry, it was nicely hidden by the shrubbery, now all the new buds and blossom had opened. Plus, it had a plastic corrugated sheet as its roof, to keep the rain out. It was a proper little hideout for the boys and their friends, and Max was looking forward to showing Danny when he arrived.

That evening, after the boys had spent a particularly good day together, they lay in bed chatting about what kind of adventures they could have in their new shelter. It seemed like the right time had come to share his magical Easter adventure, with his brother. It seemed a distant memory now; almost just a fantastic dream. But he had shared the whole experience with his best friend, Danny, and he knew it had been very very real.

The lights were out, but the summer evening was not quite dusk, and also still warm. The boys struggled to get to sleep.

'Are you asleep yet Arch?' Max whispered,

'No Max, it's too light' replied Archie, stifling a yawn.

'Shall I tell you a secret?' Max knew the answer would be yes, but asked the question anyway.

'Yeah' said Archie eagerly, sitting up in bed he turned to face his brother, yawning loudly a second time.

'First, do you believe in magic?' Max thought he'd draw the story out as long as he could.

'Course I do. Come on Max tell me the secret,' Archie was typically impatient as most 7 year olds are.

'It's something you can't tell dad, or mum. Well, not until I say you can.' Max continued. Archie yawned again. 'They probably won't believe you anyway, they are grownups after all.' Max sensed Archie's impatience growing, from the big sigh he let out as he promised not to tell, and then laid back down on his bed with a thump. Max thought he should get on with the story. 'It is something that happened to me and Danny when he came to stay at Easter. I discovered an ancient arrowhead which I think may be magic.' Max paused. No reaction so far, but he couldn't quite see Archie's face. 'Then one night we went into the park to explore, because we had seen something strange in the ring. Well, we told dad about it, but he didn't believe us, so we wanted to investigate for ourselves. It is quite complicated to explain. Arch? Archie?' There was silence from

Archie's side of the room, and when Max lifted himself up, and looked across, he saw his brother was fast asleep.

'Great' thought Max, 'shows how exciting that story was.' He laid down and closed his own eyes. Plans for the summer were forming in his mind, only one more sleep before Danny arrived for the holiday, and more adventures. Of that Max was certain.

10
DANNY IS BACK

The boys woke late on their first morning together. Danny had arrived at lunchtime the previous day, and they had just chilled at home, played games and settled Danny in. After a late bedtime, talking into the night had taken its toll. Yawning audibly, Max leaned over and poked Dan to gauge his level of consciousness. Dan groaned and rolled away.

'Gerroff,' he mumbled from beneath the duvet, then, pulling it up high under his chin, he exhaled loudly. After a minute of silence, he opened his eyes 'What time is it?' Dan mumbled.

'Dunno,' replied Max, 'but look outside, it doesn't look promising; hardly exploring weather.' Max sounded despondent; it wasn't how he had mentally planned the beginning to his holidays. Drizzly, damp and dull. The first proper full day of their fortnight together looked to be a typical British summer day. As the raindrops raced down the windowpane, Max and Dan were in no hurry to 'rise and shine.'

Movement could be heard coming from the kitchen, and the enticing smell of grilled bacon mixed with warm buttered toast wafted into the bedroom.

'Mmmmm, rain or no rain' said Dan, 'I'm still hungry. Let's go and see what your mum has on offer for breakfast.' Never known for being backwards in other people's company, Dan stretched and rolled off his inflatable mattress. He pulled on his slippers and dressing gown. 'You coming Max?' Grabbing at Max's duvet and giving it a tug, Max was forced to accompany his friend down to breakfast.

The rest of the family were already sitting round the large kitchen table, tucking into a tasty looking cooked breakfast. The kitchen floor was covered in a mixture of muddy dog's footprints and large boot prints, a sign that George had been out early.

'Good morning boys,' Martha Perry ushered both boys around the table to the vacant seats close to the heat of the range. Bozli, the family's terrier, eagerly pressed his way under the table and nuzzled his head between Max's knees. Max whispered loudly to his pet.

'Good boy, Boz, in your bed now.' After an affectionate rub on his nose, the obedient dog sloped reluctantly to his basket.

'Eggs, bacon and beans?' Martha smiled at the boys as they both nodded an affirmative. Toast was lined up in the rack and the boys helped themselves to several rounds, polishing off a large plate of eggs and bacon in very little time. Dan loved the atmosphere that surrounded a Perry family meal. There were hardly ever arguments, and the children were all included in decision-making and discussion. He felt included here, and his ideas and views mattered, however trivial. Dan envied his friend, but determined to make the most of his holiday. With clean plates they made their polite excuses and left the table to ready themselves for the day.

The boys were keen to properly plan their time together, including more time travelling adventures if possible. Once back upstairs, the boys washed and dressed, then settled back on their beds to chat, while the rain continued its relentless rampage outside. Anxious not to stir suspicion with his parents, Max suggested that any future adventures were carried out in daylight hours. Since settling in the woodland cottage, Max and his brother had become more aware of their surroundings, and had been afforded far more freedom by their parents in recent weeks. Max, however, stressed that they were still not allowed out after dark, and he didn't really want to risk getting caught breaking the rules, especially with Danny staying.

The conversation moved quickly to their past adventure, and how exactly they should plan their next move.

'The thing is Max,' said Danny, questioningly, 'how can we help this so called 'stuck' soldier, if we don't know where he is, and we don't have the lost item to get him home, when we do find him?'

'I know all that Danny,' said Max enthusiastically, 'but I have been thinking about it a lot since Easter. I wanted to talk to you about it now, I've even written a plan; it's safe in here with my arrowhead.' Max reached down under his bed and pulled out a large, quite ornate wooden box. Elaborately decorated with inlaid pieces of shell, arranged in a swirling pattern to resemble waves or flames on the lid, and similar design on the drawer at the side.

'That's new,' exclaimed Danny, 'it's a cool box, where did you get it?'

'Oh, my nanna brought it back from her last cruise; she visited India, among other places, and said when she saw it, she immediately thought of me.' Carefully Max turned the dull metal key, fixed firmly in the front of the box, and with an audible clunk the lid sprung open. He carefully reached under the open lid and pulled out a scroll of paper.

'I thought it would look like a sort of treasure map if I rolled it up like this.' Max smiled at his friend. Danny smiled back.

'Really cool mate, I like it.'

'I got the ribbon from my mum's sewing box.' Max unrolled the scroll to reveal his carefully written plan, as Danny looked on in silent anticipation. Max lifted it away from Danny's view, and began to read. 'One, we need to find the Saxon soldier,' Max drew breath, 'two, we need to find the lost item to send him home, and three, we mustn't get caught; we can trust no one.'

After reading out loud the three items on his plan, Max looked up at Danny. A notable silence stretched between them. After a minute, with no audible reaction from his friend, Max spoke.

'Well?' he said, 'what do you think?' Danny sort of smiled.

'I suppose I was expecting a...well a few more stages in the plan Max. I mean, it is ok. So far. I just think it needs a bit more detail.'

'Yeah, I know. I have done a drawing of the ring ditch, too, to show where we entered last time. I think that might help, but with the rest of the planning I really need your help. Two heads better than one, and all that? What do you reckon, as it's raining?' Max smiled hopefully and showed Danny the rough sketch he had made, with his few illegible scribbled notes. He had been worried about disappointing his friend, but Dan was more understanding than most.

'Of course. Let's do it now. The sooner we have a plan, the sooner we get out and have an adventure.' Danny's tone was positive. He always said the right things, which was why Max valued his friendship so much.

They sat down at Max's small desk to think through the next stage. It was clear that they needed to be careful, to avoid getting into trouble with the 'olds' which meant sticking to a daytime venture. They didn't really have much to go on, as far as clues to where their soldier may be, but it didn't seem likely he was stuck in 142AD. To find a new point in history Max felt they needed to enter the ring at a different place, which was the reason for the drawing.

'Well then, I think we should try the field by the Education Centre Max, you know, past where we saw the Romans last time.' Danny spoke with earnest. 'It is a lot further around the ring clockwise, if you imagine the circle of the ring ditch as a giant clock.' Danny's enthusiasm grew as the idea blossomed. Max nodded in agreement. 'Then further round should mean more recent in time.'

'Or longer ago,' said Max, 'we might end up in dinosaur time!?' Both boys laughed, but looked apprehensively at one another, as their smiles faded.

'Well, we don't know 'til we try, Max,' as ever Danny was the positive energy in their plan, and his upbeat vibe gave Max the confidence to agree.

The boys jotted their final plans onto the end of Max's original scroll, then sat back with a sigh. The rain still fell heavily from the sky and the grey clouds filled the view from Max's bedroom window. An adventure on this day, looked exceedingly unlikely.

11
A NEW ADVENTURE

The boys woke early the next morning. It might have been the excitement of being together again. Maybe it was the fact that it was the school holidays, and of course it is well known that children always wake early when they don't need to. Or possibly, it was the anticipation of a new adventure that had forced them from their sleep early that morning. Yet it was none of these. It was a bright, warm beam of sunshine, streaming in through somewhat grubby windows, straight on to the faces of the two sleeping boys, which roused them a little after dawn. Dozing on and off for another hour or so, Max eventually found he had to get up to visit the bathroom, and as he carefully squeezed past Danny's make shift bed, he noticed his friend open one eye. When he returned to his bed, Danny was standing by the window, his dressing gown hanging over his shoulders.

'This is more like it Max,' Danny smiled and turned to his friend, 'much better weather for adventures!'

'It is lovely and sunny,' said Max, joining his friend at the window, 'I really hope it stays like this. We will have to go out early, just in case the weather changes.'

'I agree. Straight after breakfast?' Danny, as usual, was thinking of food first.

'But breakfast won't be for a while yet, Dan. After all it is only...' Max peered over to his clock radio to check the time '...still only 6.42 am. I think we will have to check through our plan again. If we start moving about now, we might wake the others, and if that happens my mum will not be happy!'

The boys got back into their respective beds, and grabbed the box where the plan was carefully stored. The plan and corresponding map had been developed further during the rainy afternoon of the previous day, and the boys had enjoyed adding landmarks and colour to the map. Max had also placed the most valuable tool of time travel; the Stone Age arrowhead, into the new box with the plan. Excitement bubbled as they chatted over their simple plan. It really wasn't very complex, they just needed to get back out into the park and explore.

At about 8 o'clock, there was movement in the house. Max's dad George had a day off, so had not gone out as early as he usually did, but the dog still woke at the same time every day, so George rarely enjoyed a long lie in. The boys slipped into their dressing gowns and slippers, and headed out onto the landing to check the lie of the land. Jess was now in her own tiny bedroom, adjacent to her parent's room. It had originally been the box room where all the removal crates had been stored after their move. Now cleared it provided adequate space for Jess. Archie had also just moved in to his own room, which had been a big step for Max's younger brother, as he had always shared with his older sibling in their old house. His newly decorated 'dinosaur room' as it became known, was right up

Archie's street, and from the minute he saw the giant dinosaur stencils, he fell in love with it. Max was just glad to have his room back to himself, especially now he had a friend to stay.

In the big kitchen George was pouring a cup of tea. He was clearly surprised to see the two boys up so early.

'Couldn't you boys sleep?' he joked. He pulled his chair out, dragging it against the stone flooring.

'Oh, well we did have an early night Dad, because of the rubbish weather yesterday.' Max tried to sound casual, but unwarranted guilt filled his voice.

'And we really don't want to waste any of this lovely day, Mr Perry,' said Danny, perhaps a little too eagerly. George, however, had no reason to suspect anything untoward. He waved them towards the breakfast table, where cereal and juice were already lined up.

'There's toast too, if you want to help yourselves. You know where everything is Max, so help Danny to find whatever he would like. Don't be scared of it, boys, there is always plenty to go around.'

'Thanks Mr Perry,' Danny sounded less hesitant.

'Yes Dad, I will.' Max smiled as he put a couple of slices into the toaster. 'Help yourself to cereal Dan, while I do the toast.' Finishing his breakfast, George put his jacket on and grabbed the dog's lead; Bozli eager at his heels, followed happily.

'I'll see you later boys. Don't get up to any mischief now.'
George winked at Danny, then left by the back door.
The boys had the kitchen to themselves. Once George was clearly
out of sight, they gobbled up the last of their toast, and not waiting to
digest their hurried breakfast, shot back upstairs to get dressed.

The big house had two bathrooms, and the children generally used
the family bathroom, rather than the en-suite attached to the adult's
bedroom. The boys could wash and dress quickly without disturbing
the rest of the family, and with the valued contents of his special
box, tightly within Max's grasp, they headed back downstairs.

George had not returned with the dog, which meant there was a
danger of bumping into him on their walk, yet the boys were itching
to get out, and thought carefully of the consequences, should they
meet him on their way to the ring.

'Well Max, if we see him while we are out, we just say we
are exploring. You will need to hide the map and plan, but that is
all.' Dan was convincing. They had a feeling of guilt, but needn't as
they hadn't done anything wrong. The feeling was a mixture of
excitement and guilt, with a little fear thrown in, but the boys agreed
excitement outweighed anything bad. They put on their light jackets
and training shoes, then left by the back door. It was just after 9 am.

Deciding to take the most direct route to the ring ditch, they avoided
the Yew Tree Circle, but it meant using the main footpath for part of

the way. They passed an elderly couple slowly walking with their grey faced Labrador. The dog was also clearly in his twilight years, but the couple Max knew were regulars to the park, and he smiled a nod as they approached. They didn't see George and reached the ring ditch in under 5 minutes. Walking slower now along the foot of the ditch, they passed the area where they had exited the ditch on their previous adventure.

'My heart's beating faster Max, is yours?' said Danny.

'I know what you mean, Dan, I feel a bit like I can't breathe properly; like I have to keep taking a deep breath just to feel normal.' Max was having trouble explaining exactly how he felt, but Dan knew what he meant. 'Let's keep going round until we get level with the Education Centre. It is quite a bit further round the ring. We must stick to our plan!'

'Yep, I'm with that,' said Dan, and they quickened their step.

When they reached the bank, parallel to the Education Centre, they stopped and looked up. For some reason the ditch was much deeper at this point, and the bank quite steep. There was a large beech tree on the ditch side of the fence, but barbed wire behind it. The boys looked at one another, pausing briefly, then clambered up the bank, clutching at bare roots and undergrowth to aid their ascent. Max got there first, and with one hand firmly gripping a low hanging branch, he held out his free hand to Danny. Eventually they both stood at the top of the bank, next to the giant beech, but in front of a thick privet and hawthorn hedge, backed by a wire fence which was topped with the barbed wire.

'Great!' exclaimed Danny sarcastically. 'This isn't going to be as easy an entrance as the last one was, someone certainly doesn't encourage intruders!' He looked at Max for inspiration, which for a change, Max was able to supply.

'Well, we will walk along a bit, looking for any gaps at all in the vegetation. Look low down, because the wire fence is old and broken in places.' Max knew this as he and Archie regularly spent time in the Education Centre paddock when George was working there. He began to walk along the hedge line, careful not to slip back into the ring ditch. 'Did you know, Danny, that Roman skeletons have been found along here?' They continued very slowly until Max crouched down by a potential entrance.

'No, Max, I didn't know skeletons had been found here. I am not sure I want to know, just at this minute!' He joined Max and crouched down. 'But I think we can just about squeeze through here, which is what I guess you are thinking?'

'Yes Dan, I think it is our best bet. I've got the arrowhead here in my pocket, and the map too, so are you ready to go?' Max had an unusual confidence in his voice.

'I am. Let's go!' Danny grinned to his friend, as they ducked down, and pushed through the undergrowth together.

12
MEETING CHARLIE

It was a struggle getting through the privet, without being spiked and scratched. Max was through first and dusting himself down as Danny struggled to his feet. They both caught their breath, then turned to face the Education Centre building.

'Oh Max,' said Danny in a low whisper, 'I don't think *he* is very pleased to see us!' Max turned in the direction of Danny's view to see a rather large black stallion staring back at them. Although there was no visible steam coming out of his nostrils, had he been a cartoon character, they were both sure there would have been.

'Yes. Right. Ok what now?' A little flustered, Max looked around for an obvious solution to their problem. 'I've got it.' Still speaking in whispers, Max issued Danny with the instruction that on the count of three they should make a run for a wooden gate to the left and behind the disgruntled looking horse. The boys took off after Max's count, running quickly to the gate and scrambling over with ease. Catching their breath, the boys laughed together for a moment, then gradually started to take in their surroundings properly for the first time.

'Have we time travelled Max?' asked Danny, less familiar with the park Max lived and played in on a daily basis.

'We certainly have Dan, but I'm not sure where we have ended up. At least it isn't pre-historic, I wasn't quite sure what we would do if we came face to face with a Tyrannosaurus Rex!'

'They didn't exist on our continent Max, but I know what you mean! What is here that you recognise then?' Both boys looked around. There was a large cedar tree over to their right, and a stable block for the horses, adjacent to the field they had just run through.

'Well, I recognise that tree,' said Max hoping it meant they hadn't travelled back very far, 'but the Education Centre has gone...well, not gone, those stables are in its place, and,' Max stopped for a moment, 'and that massive mansion house means it is before 1954, because it was almost completely demolished in 1954. I'm sure that was the date, and it was fairly derelict then anyway, like it is now.' At that point they heard the rumbling of wheels on the cobbled path, and the clip clop of horse's hooves. An ornate carriage pulled by two beautiful chestnut mares, and driven by two men who were sat proudly and smartly at the front of the carriage, came around the corner and up the drive. The boys ducked behind a tree out of view, as the carriage passed them and disappeared through an archway behind the main house. To the side of the house there was a courtyard, and before they had a chance to move away from their hiding place, a door in the main house opened onto the courtyard and a girl carrying a large basket of washing came through it. It was only then that they saw the washing line tied around the trunk of the tree they were hiding behind, and before they knew it, the girl had reached their end of her line and had dropped her basket to start hanging out the clean sheets. They shuffled back, not knowing whether they had been seen, and in their hurry to conceal themselves further, had inadvertently drawn attention to themselves.

'Hey' called the girl, 'is someone there?' She stood looking in their direction, not moving. She wore a long black dress almost to the ground, covered with a frilly white apron, and a funny kind of mop hat on her head. She looked friendly enough. Older than them, the boys thought, but not much older.

'What shall we do?' whispered Danny.

The girl called out again 'I know you're there; show yerselves, or I'll call the master and he'll bring the dogs.' The boys looked worriedly at each other at this point, and nodded. Then slowly they came out of their hiding place to face the young girl.

'Oh my,' she said, 'I was thinking there might be poachers hidden in those bushes, but you're nowt but a couple o' young lads, out for mischief no doubt?' She smiled, and her face softened. 'You friends of Master Albert?' she questioned the boys.

'Er..no, not exactly,' Danny hesitated a response, 'we...we were just out exploring.'

'Exploring eh, hmm, funny clothes you're wearing. Come closer, I don't bite. My name is Molly, what's yours?'

'Oh, I'm Max and this is my friend Danny,' relaxing a bit, the boys smiled back at the girl they now knew as Molly.

'Funny names too. And what is that strange metal thing on your sweater? And young Max and you too young Danny, how on earth did you manage to get past the master of the gate? No one usually gets past old Henry.' She chuckled and continued to hang out her washing. Hesitating yet again, and shuffling a bit on the spot, Max was the first to speak.

'We didn't come in through the main gate Molly, we came through those bushes over there,' he turned and pointed to the other side of the Education Centre paddock, where the large black horse now casually chewed at the grass.

'Yeah' piped up Danny, 'and that metal thing on Max's jumper is a zip. You know, to undo it, so he can take it off.' He grinned at Max, pleased that he knew something an older girl didn't.

'A zip, did you say? Never heard o' one of those before. I bet that came from America. Anyhow, you boys shouldn't be on the estate without an invitation; if Lord Greyford should spot you, I wouldn't like to say what might happen.'

At that point a small boy emerged from the door at the side of the great house Molly had used. He wandered out into the courtyard area, and looked to be approaching. He wore a flat cap and short trousers; a very scruffy white shirt and waistcoat.

'He looks like I did when I dressed up for Victorian day at school,' said Danny, taking a step towards the boy. The boy then hesitated and paused, he had clearly spotted the two boys and knew something wasn't quite the same as usual.

'Hey Charlie, don't be afraid, come over here and meet two friends of mine.' Molly giggled again. The boy Charlie, continued until he almost reached the washing line where Molly stood. 'Charlie, meet Max and Danny,' she pointed to the boys as she introduced them to the scruffy young Charlie. He was shorter than both boys, with dirty black marks on his forehead, and one on his cheek. His held out his hand to Max.

'How do?' said Charlie, looking down.

'Oh, how do you do too?' said Max, taking Charlie's hand, and giving it a firm shake, despite its grubbiness.
Danny wanted to get in on the action too.

'Hello Charlie, I'm Danny, very pleased to meet you.'

'Likewise,' said Charlie, looking a little less afraid.

'How old are you Charlie?' Danny guessed at around eight or nine. The boy was small and quite thin. His cheeks, under the dirt, were gaunt, and generally Danny thought the boy looked fairly undernourished.

'I'm eleven years old.' Charlie looked back towards the house, 'I should get back.' He looked worried.

'Oh why so soon, will your mum be worried?' Max spoke with genuine interest. He knew how hard it was to get out and play himself, without worrying his mum.

'Oh no Max, Charlie has no mother, or father come to that. Charlie needs to get back to work, he only came out for a 5-minute fresh air break. He often pops out when I'm hanging the washing out, to help me,' Molly looked caringly towards Charlie, 'don't you Charlie. You help me when you can?' she repeated, as if she was worried he may not agree. He nodded.

'We help one another where we can.' The small boy looked back to Molly.

'Work?' exclaimed Danny. 'But you are only eleven years old, for goodness sake, it's positively Victorian making you do jobs!'

It was at this point, it dawned on the two boys, the relevance of Danny's statement.

'Victorian. That's it, isn't it Max?' Danny turned to his friend while the others looked on puzzled. He then turned back to Molly. 'Molly, is Victoria your queen?'

'What kind of daft question is that Danny. You know as well as I do that our good Queen Victoria has reigned for the past 24 years, and I think she probably has a good many years left in her yet.'

'Yeah, 40' said Max under his breath as it began to dawn on him exactly where in history they had been transported to. Unconsciously he put his hand to his pocket, and as before, a warmth from the arrowhead could be felt through his jeans.

'What was that you said Max?' Molly hung out the last bed sheet to dry, then picked up her basket. Before he had a chance to respond, there was rumbling from the archway and the horse and carriage moved slowly out, along the cobbled path, straight towards the small group.

'Hey, lads, you mustn't be seen, quickly follow us back into the house to hide, before the carriage driver sees you. Stand behind me as we make our way back.' Molly moved quickly, and without giving any thought to the consequences of entering the old Manor House on a Victorian summers day, the boys followed closely. Ducking in through the open door between Charlie and Molly, the boys tumbled down two concrete steps just inside the entrance, but at least they had avoided being spotted. Or had they?

13
INSIDE THE MANOR

'Oh my, that was close,' Molly spoke with relief as she helped Danny to his feet. 'I don't think they saw us, but that was old Reynolds in the carriage. He can be a funny old sort sometimes, and eagle eyes he has.'

The small group moved through the enclosed brick entrance hall into a kitchen, when suddenly a sharp rap on the back door made everyone jump. Molly looked at Charlie, then putting a finger to her lips, waved him away in the direction of a large wooden door. Then, once they were out of sight, she returned to the servant's entrance to open the back door. Sure enough, Reynolds stood tall before her.

'Young Molly. Did I see you allowing people into the great house just now?' he frowned, and paused for her response.

'Of course not sir, oh no,' Molly was frantically trying to think of an explanation. 'I had my large basket, and of course Charlie was with me, he helped me hang out the washing. No one else sir, you must have been mistaken. Our running, may have blurred your vision sir, may I suggest?' Reynolds didn't look convinced, and peered over her shoulder to get a good look in the kitchen.

'Please do come in sir,' invited Molly, in the knowledge that the boys had by now hidden in the cellar stairwell.

'Oh, well, no you are right, I must have been mistaken. I should probably look to get a new pair of spectacles.' Reynolds half smiled, and turned to return to the carriage. Molly closed the door with a deep sigh of relief.

'That was a close call,' she thought.

Returning to the kitchen, the boys certainly were hidden from view. She opened the large ledge and brace door, and peered down into the darkness of the cellar steps. In a loud whisper, she called to them.

'Boys, the coast is clear. Reynolds has gone on his way.' Muffled footsteps could be heard from quite a way down into the darkness, getting louder as they approached the exit. 'Is all well?' Molly's kindness was evident, even to the boys she hardly knew.

'Yes, but I have to get back to work now,' said Charlie anxiously. He squeezed past Danny and Max, to emerge from the cellar. 'I will be back at 12 mid-day, should you still be here then, you can sit with me as I take my lunch.' He then hurried away through another door leading out of the large kitchen.

'You can stay here, if you like?' said Molly. 'I will get you a candle. The cellar is dim and cold, but no one will find you there.' Molly too needed to get on with her work. 'I'll tell Charlie to come and find you here then?' She didn't appear to be giving the boys much choice, and handed a candlestick holder containing a tall white candle burning with a large yellow flame. Then off she went.

'Oh great, what now?' said Max, clearly unhappy with the arrangement. Notoriously the less adventurous of the pair, he was starting to get cold feet. Danny on the other hand, was revelling in the new experiences generated by their time travelling.

'We're ok Max. We can go down and explore a bit, now there is some light, then when Charlie comes back, we can sit down and chat to him. Tell him where we've come from and why we are here.' Always so upbeat, Max wished he was as confident as his friend.

'Yeah. Well it doesn't look like we have a lot of choice really, does it?' Max sighed, resigning himself to the fact. They turned and retraced their steps down into the cold stone cellar. A dusty, fruity smell wafted in on a draft, where a chink of light stole through a gap in the stones. The cellar was shelved with narrow wooden slats, and glass bottles lined the top shelf laying on their sides. The middle shelf had wider stone glazed bottles, sitting upright, together with empty wooden crates. The boys gazed in silence for a while, as the dust particles circled in the air they breathed. Danny placed the lit candle on the wooden shelf and turned back to his friend.

'Well Max, we can either sit here and mope for an hour or so, or we can explore a bit down here.' His voice lifted at this last suggestion. 'My choice is to keep exploring, and the cellar probably goes further under the big house than we can see by the light of this small candle. Come on Max, be brave.' Danny chuckled to his friend, and by the combined light of a dim candle and the chink of sunlight, he could see a smile on Max's face.

'OK, Dan. Where now?' relented Max with a sigh.

'This way,' said Danny grabbing the candlestick holder, and walking towards the darkest point in the cellar. Max followed. The space was cold and damp, and full of cobwebs. The floor was covered in a thick layer of detritus, built up over years and years. It created a crunchy cushion beneath their feet. Max tried not to look down too closely, but equally he tried his best not to look up either, blocking thoughts of the horrible things that might be peering at him out of the darkness. With Danny out in front, Max pushed on to keep up.

'Which way now?' Max raised the question, as their short walk along the dark cellar tunnel resulted in a split. Two tunnels. After walking gingerly, in an uncomfortable, slightly hunched over position, for less than a few minutes, the boys had a decision to make. As both tunnels looked identical, and both very dark, it was decided literally by the toss of a coin, and as Danny scrabbled about on the floor for the ten pence piece he had dropped, he made an interesting discovery.

'Hey, Max, look at this.' Danny held the candle down at floor level. There was a clear pathway in the dirt, as if one tunnel had been used recently. Danny held up the candle, where it threw a small amount of light into the narrow space; something or someone had definitely used this tunnel quite recently. 'Don't worry about what the coin says, let's take this one anyway, I want to see what is stored down here,' said Danny enthusiastically. In truth, Max was feeling uneasy again by the whole experience and was thinking it was time to return to the kitchens, and some proper fresh air.

Without time to air his views, however, Danny had set off at a slightly quicker pace, down the left-hand tunnel and Max had no option in the darkness but to follow.

'Wait for me then Danny,' whispered Max as he quickened his step to catch up. They continued in the darkness, following the track in the dirt on the cellar floor, when their journey ended abruptly. A large wooden door blocked their passage any further. Danny held the light up to the door to view it in detail. There was something very odd about the door, which Max spotted immediately.

'It doesn't have a handle of any kind,' he observed, and he put his hand up and gave it a gentle push. Nothing happened, the door was shut fast.

'I thought I heard something then Max,' whispered Danny 'be really quiet and listen.' Both boys stood in silence. There it was again. 'Did you hear that Max? A kind of snorting sound.' The boys looked at each other in the limited shadow of the candle's flame.

'I did,' Max's voice was so quiet it was almost inaudible, 'I think it sounds like someone snoring, and it seems to be coming from the other side of the door.'

Together, instinctively, both boys stepped forward and pressed one ear up against the door's heavy oak panelling. It was cold against their cheeks; musty smelling and damp. There it was again. Definite snoring, but then something else which startled them somewhat. From behind the closed door another voice; young, and well spoken, but abrupt.

'*Soldier, wake up. I have water for you. Wake up I say.*' The sound of the disembodied voice, resounding through the solid door was too much for Max to bear.

'That's it Dan, I'm out of here,' he cried as he turned to leave the tunnel. Danny followed, quickly catching his friend. They walked briskly back to the point where the tunnel had split, then back on to the main cellar. At last they reached the shelved cellar area, where the small amount of light filtering in felt like bright sunlight after the pitch darkness of the tunnel. There, they sank down onto the cellar steps, to catch their breath. Danny was the first to speak.

'Did you hear what was said Max?' Danny's voice was quiet.

'I think so, yes.' Max was hesitant.

'So you heard the word *soldier*?' There was a pause.

'I think I heard someone say '*soldier, wake up*', is that what you heard?' Max's voice was slow, and uncertain. Danny looked at him.

'That is exactly what I heard. Oh boy Max, do you know what I think?' Danny could hardly contain the growing excitement in his voice.

'What Danny?'

With a huge grin on his face, Danny stood up, excitedly.

'I think we've just found our missing Saxon soldier!'

14
GOING HOME

Out in the bright sunshine, Danny and Max headed for the shade of the tree where they had entered the 19th century, and sat down. Danny was anxious that they did not waste any more of the time they had with Charlie, and as soon as they saw him appear at the kitchen door, Danny gestured to him to join them. Trying not to draw too much attention to their presence, Danny did not call out. Charlie saw him wave and was with them in seconds.

'Hiya Chaz, come and sit down here with us,' his informality with Charlie didn't appear to bother the young boy, who sat between them, and opened a paper wrapped parcel, containing a piece of bread, and a chunk of cheese.

'Hello again Danny.' Charlie took a bite of his cheese and pulled a piece of bread from the hunk in the paper.

'We have loads to talk to you about, Charlie,' Max had at last managed to get in a word. 'Firstly though, we can't really stay very much longer, but we want to know if you can tell us something?' A question clear in his tone. Charlie looked from one boy to the other.

'Yes,' said Danny, 'we think we made an important discovery while we were down in that dirty cellar, and we need your help with something really important. And I mean *really* important Charlie.' His voice was pleading, and Charlie looked with open eyes, but a full mouth. He couldn't speak, so just nodded. 'Do you know whether there is someone living down there?'

At this, Max frowned at Danny and shook his head. They had not really thought to plan what they were going to do, or say next. Max had been keen to get back home, whilst Danny wanted to stay a bit longer to meet Charlie again. As usual Danny had got his own way, but the one thing they had agreed on was that they wouldn't mention the voices they had heard.

'No, what Danny means is, is there a way through the tunnel where it seems to be blocked? It looks like people go through there, but the door has no handle.' Max wanted more time with Danny to properly plan what they were going to do next, and he was worried about scaring Charlie off if they were too inquisitive.

'Well, there is a door, yes. We knock and then must move away. It is opened from the other side. I don't know if there is anyone there, but I have occasionally been told to take a plate of bread and cheese, or a glass of ale. I have to knock, and leave the food by the door.' Charlie seemed quite happy to talk about it. He was more relaxed than when they had met the first time. Max and Danny exchanged an excited glance.

Who tells you to take food down there Charlie? How often do you have to do that?' Danny wanted to know everything, but Max was by now getting a little fidgety. Charlie looked to Danny, a frown creasing his forehead.

'I am not sure Danny. It is usually Molly who gives me the food, but why are you asking me this?' He took another bite of bread and cheese, looking a little more concerned than when he had first sat down.

'Oh nothing to worry about,' jumped in Max, before Danny could reply. 'We really do need to be going home now actually, but it has been great to meet you Charlie, hasn't it Danny?' Max looked to his friend and stood up to leave. Danny didn't move. He wasn't finished with his questions, and he wasn't ready to leave, whatever Max said.

'Well Charlie,' said Danny 'I think we could be really good friends, you and Molly, with Max and I.' Charlie smiled at Danny. He had never had a proper friend before.

'I'd like that Danny, and you Max, I'd really like to be your friend.' Max looked pleadingly to Danny, who understood that 'look' and reluctantly stood up.

'We will be back to see you again soon Charlie, I promise,' said Danny. Charlie smiled and his new friends smiled back. Max looked at his watch, and grabbed hold of Danny by the shoulder.

'We must go now Dan,' he said, 'we have been out quite a long time.' They turned and both crept around the large beech tree towards the gate. The horse was no longer visible in the paddock. It looked like a simple clear run. Looking back towards Charlie, they could see he was engrossed in his lunch, and not interested in the direction the boys were taking.

'Ok Dan, ready to make a run for it?' Max's question was their instruction to go. Dan gave a brief nod, and within seconds both boys had jumped over the gate and were running across the grass towards the far side of the paddock, without a backwards glance, straight into the thorny shrubbery from where they had emerged about two hours earlier. Marginally out of breath, the boys ducked down, and just as they had done on their earlier time travelling adventures, wriggled back through the undergrowth at the exact point they had entered it. Dirty and dishevelled the boys pulled themselves to their feet and descended the steep bank of the ditch. Max looked at his wristwatch and smiled.

'It has happened again Dan, my watch says we've only been out for 10 minutes.' The boys laughed, the oddities of time travel no longer puzzled them. Max put his hand to his pocket. The arrowhead was still safely stored, together with their map. They were by now seasoned time travellers. They pulled their jackets straight and brushed off the leaf debris attached to various parts of their clothing.

'It may only say 10 minutes on your watch Max, but I'm starving. Watching Charlie eat that fresh chunk of bread was almost too much. Let's go and see what your mum can offer us.' Danny took the lead and strode forwards into the ring ditch. How many more adventures could this ancient Iron Age ring ditch hold? How many more mysteries? The boys picked up their pace, and jogged back around the ring and along the dusty track back to the cottage.

15
MAKING PLANS

As with their earlier adventures, the two boys were glad to be home in an environment they knew and understood. There was something about time travelling that made those who experienced it, question themselves. It was unbelievable. A thing of story books, and the boys had to reassure one another they had really been there; really had seen the things they had seen, smelt the smells, had the conversations. *They* knew they were real, but reassurance made them feel more comfortable with the idea. Nevertheless, the afternoon was one to rest after the excitement of the morning. After grabbing a cereal bar from the kitchen, the boys trundled upstairs to vegetate in Max's room with some electronic gadgets for company.

After an hour in front of the tv, followed by a big pile of sandwiches and crisps for lunch, the boys were restless again. They had unfinished business and their mission to help an unknown soldier from the past was becoming a reality at last. More plans were needed, and the boys agreed they had to talk about it away from uninvited ears.

'Let's go out to the new den in the woods.' Max had renewed enthusiasm; he got up and put his lunch plate into the kitchen sink. Dan followed his friend out of the back door, and around the side of the house. The sun was bright and warm on their faces. The den stood a little dishevelled by the blustery weather that had been prevalent earlier in the year, but was mainly intact. Max pushed back the make shift door and squeezed in to the small cosy space. Danny spoke as he entered the den.

'I've been thinking,' he took a deep breath.

'So have I Dan' said Max quickly, 'so before you decide the next move, we have to be in agreement. I think you worried Charlie earlier, by hassling him about the soldier.'

'I didn't hassle him,' said Dan defensively, 'I just thought we had to grab the opportunity to get as much information as possible.'

'Yes Dan, but I have had an idea which would mean we don't need to go back in time again, just yet.'

'Go on,' said Dan, not sounding convinced that his friend could deliver anything remotely as interesting for the afternoon, as going back to the Victorian age!

'Well, I have thought about two things. Firstly, my dad has a book which shows a plan of the old house, as it was. Secondly, there is a box of bits in our cellar which came out of an old Victorian pit, which is on the other side of the ring. It may have clues in it.'

'What sort of clues?' Dan sounded sceptical.

'I don't know yet, but in films there are always clues when it comes to a mystery, or proper investigation of one kind or another, so it has to be worth a look. Anyway, I have my notebook. Let's make a list, or a plan of what we will do next. Then we can go and play on the trampoline with Archie for a while. I did promise he could spend a bit of time with us this afternoon.' Max sounded quite in charge of the situation, and for once, Danny was happy to listen.

The first thing they agreed was that they needed the book with the old lay out of the house, so Max nipped back indoors to get it. All the books were on the large bookcase at the top of the winding staircase, in a very clear order, and it took him no time at all to retrieve it from the top shelf, and return to the den.

'We may be able to find another way in to the cellar to have a look at the lay out. Once we can understand the tunnels, it will be easier to go back and get the soldier when we return to the Victorian time. I know my dad talks about the bat tower; he goes down every winter to check on the bats. I think it links to the cellar.' Max was on fire. Ideas were just flowing, and his confidence growing as he voiced them.

The boys opened the big book entitled 'The History of Greyford Hall and Gardens' where they found a sketch of the grounds inside the front cover. Turning the dusty yellowing pages carefully, they found Chapter 4 had more detailed architects drawings of the main house. Finally, the last page in the chapter was the cellar map.

'Look what it says here, Max. The servants used tunnels to avoid being seen in the big house, by the gentry. It also says some deliveries were taken straight to the cellar from the road.'

'That's it! That's the bat tunnel, right by the road.' Max stood up excitedly.

'Ok mate, sit down,' said Danny, calming his friend. 'We need to look at this first, then the box of bits in your cellar.'

'Oh, and look at this bit Danny. Oh boy, oh wow, geez!' Max really couldn't contain his excitement as he read on through chapter 4.

'What is it then?' Danny squealed. 'Let me in on the excitement.'

'Well, look at this long tunnel here, see?' Max pointed, jabbing at the page, and Danny looked on, none the wiser. 'It looks like; yes, I'm sure it links up with *our* cellar. The tunnel goes all the way to a building they used to call 'Stewards Cottage' and I know that this house we live in, used to be lived in by the gardener to the big house, as late as the 1900's because my mum looked at the census.' As the boys pored over the map, the talking stopped. Thinking started in earnest, and the outline of serious plans began to form in their heads. Were Max and Danny about to take their big adventure one step further? A while passed then Danny spoke.

'I think we need to go down into your cellar, without delay.' Danny got up this time. 'It is still early. We can check the box of bits out, and the cellar too. Then we can play on the trampoline for a bit.'

'Yes, I'm good with that. I need to get the cellar key first. Come on.' Max pushed back through the make shift door of the den, with the book tucked under his arm. The impulse to get going again, meant they still hadn't really discussed plans. The adventure seemed to be taking over, and they had no choice but to follow!

After safely retrieving the cellar key, the boys made their way around to the back of the house, where Max slid the big iron key into the lock in the cellar door. It turned easily, and the door swung open inwards. Dark inside, Max leant forward and switched on a light. The benefits of the modern age. No candles needed here. Well, not yet, anyway.

'Careful Dan, remember the steps are very steep,' warned Max as he took the lead and entered the cellar. The smell of dampness was not dissimilar to that of the 19th century cellar. But they turned the corner at the bottom of the steps and came to an abrupt halt. They were met by free standing shelving, some holding bottles of wine, and some empty. The box of finds dug up from the Victorian pit, sat right on the edge.

'Well there isn't a tunnel here now Max,' said Danny, stating the obvious.

'I know that Dan, I have been down here before. I just wondered if I may have missed something on my earlier visits; I never took much notice before.' At that, Max got down on his knees and looked under the shelving. The lighting was poor, but Max felt sure he could see a very dark patch that was literally under the stairway. After a minute or so, straining his eyes, he kneeled up.

'I think it is here Dan. I am pretty sure these shelves are in front of a blocked-up tunnel, and it leads back in the direction of the big house.' Max took a deep breath. 'And if I am right, then we are very close to our next adventure, my friend.'

16
VISITING THE PIT

Archie enjoyed the company of his brother and Danny, and they had played for over an hour on the trampoline. They bounced a few balls to one another in the rare July sunshine. When Archie announced that he had had enough and wanted to go back inside, Max and Danny smiled at each other. Max kindly helped him climb down off the trampoline, and Archie ran back indoors.

Alone again, and at only 3 o'clock on a bright afternoon, the boys were fired up for adventure once more.

The box of finds from the Victorian pit, had been removed from the cellar by the boys earlier that day, and was waiting in the den for them to go through it thoroughly. Now was their opportunity. They quickly vacated the trampoline, donned their shoes and headed to their woodland retreat.

'What do you think we will find Max?' Danny hadn't a clue what to expect.

'Well, I know there are bottles and jars, which can be quite valuable now to collectors. I don't really know exactly what we will find, but it is quite interesting,' Max spoke enthusiastically, 'if you like old stuff, that is,' he added.

This is where the boys' interests differed. Danny wasn't interested in old bits, or antiques of any kind, whereas Max loved all the traditional collectables, and bottles in particular. Unusual for an 11-year-old boy, but Max had many collections, and this was just one of them. His hobby meant he also enjoyed metal detecting, and his small coin collection was one of his favourites.

'I had been thinking Dan,' said Max in lifted spirits, 'that we could take my metal detector and a spade down to the site of the pit. Just for something different to do.'

Dan smiled 'Whatever you think, Max.'

'Well, have you got a better idea Dan? No?' Max spoke assertively. 'So come on, let's go through the box now, and then take it from there?'

Dan nodded to his friend, a little disappointed that they wouldn't be testing the arrowhead again that day, but happy just the same.

The box; an old wooden crate, had been filled very carefully, with mainly glass bottles, of all shapes, colours and sizes. There were also some jars, and old pottery lids. As the boys delved into the crate, selecting those items most appealing, Danny began to show more interest.

'Hey Max, look at this one.' Danny lifted a dark coloured jar and waved it in Max's face. It had a short squat body and a long neck. 'A Marmite jar,' he exclaimed, then 'oh no, it says Bovril, similar though, but with a longer neck I think.'

This observation by Danny impressed Max.

'See' said Max 'they can be interesting. That one is a Bovril jar, and it's Victorian. Most of these bottles are from around the 1890s, so just a bit later than Charlie & Molly's time. I can't see anything Saxon though. Mind you, I can't think what we would be looking for that the soldier could have lost anyway, can you?' Max looked at Danny, who shrugged his shoulders.

'No, I can't,' said Danny as he got up, losing interest as quickly as he'd gained it. 'Clearly it must be something Saxon soldiers had. Shall we go now?'

'Yes, let's.' Max got up and joined Dan, 'I'll go and get my metal detector. It will be daylight for a few more hours, so we could make a discovery yet today.'

Armed with the detector, two trowels, a cotton bag with drinks and a snack, and a canvas p.e bag in which to place any finds, the boys headed down the garden path. Martha was gathering her washing in as they passed her, and looked over with a smile.

'Where are you two adventurers off to, all loaded up like that?'

'Oh, just to do a bit of treasure hunting,' said Max lightly.

'Go carefully boys, dinner will be ready at 6.' Turning to pick up her washing basket, the boys grinned at one another, and took off through the garden gate.

It was a short walk past the orchard, and that point in the ring where they had first entered the past; the point where they had wriggled through the shrubbery, and stumbled upon Roman Britain. A little further along the regular tree lined path, they quickened their pace, excitement building.

'I can't wait to start digging,' said Danny eagerly, 'can I use the detector first?' Max smiled.

'This way' he said, and they left the path, edging along the side of a field, where cattle stood idly grazing. A sparse hedge, neatly trimmed, had a strip of electric fencing running along its length.

'Careful you don't touch the white tape Dan,' Max warned, 'and just follow me. We need to climb over the gate you can see up in front, at the very end of this field.' Max continued to move purposefully in front as Dan quickened to keep up.

At the gate, they both clambered over, careful to avoid some rusty barbed wire which clung to the top edge, menacingly. Once clear, they both brushed themselves down.

'This is it,' said Max proudly. Danny stared. A fairly steep slope faced them, leading down into a shrub covered pit, hidden within the woods. Max started to clamber down, carefully choosing the correct foot holds until he had safely reached the bottom. Dan followed, more quickly, noticing there was a great deal of broken glass, bottles and crockery pieces poking through the ivy-covered ground.

'Don't put your hands down, if you can help it Dan,' Max said helpfully, 'because there is a lot of broken glass lying around.'

'You don't say,' said Dan sarcastically as he joined his friend. 'What now?'

Danny wasn't sure what he had been expecting; he guessed a secret store of treasure hidden in the woods, but this really was a pit. Initially he felt a pang of disappointment, until Max turned his metal detector on, and it immediately emitted a loud beeping, which pulled his thoughts back to the job in hand.

'Right, what do I do?' Danny was keen to get started.

'I've set it, so you just need to sweep it across the ground, like this.' Max demonstrated, with a slow considered stroke. Danny took the detector from his friend and copied the action.
The hunting now began with earnest. Would the boys find treasure, tin cans, or even the missing link?

17
THE DIG

Danny had started the search enthusiastically, feeling sure he would set the metal detector's alarm off within seconds. And he did. After a frantic few minutes searching for his trowel which he had discarded as he clambered into the pit, his eventual digging had revealed a crumpled up, 1980's yoghurt pot lid. Not put off, he continued to scan the area with Max looking on, hands on hips.

'Shall I have a go now?' Max anxious not to miss out, yet not wanting to appear pushy, edged towards Danny.

'Just let me keep going for a tad longer please Max. You can do this any time.' Danny wasn't ready to give up yet.

After 20 minutes of searching, and begrudgingly taking turns to use the detector, the sum of their hoard comprised an old coke lid, a Fanta ring pull, two more yoghurt pot lids, and a very nice white jar complete with its decomposing metal lid. Max thought it was a 20th century ladies face cream pot. Dan was quite impressed at his friend's knowledge. However, nothing the boys considered to be treasure, and nothing that could conceivably have been lost by a Saxon soldier.

They sat down on a clear part of the bank, taking care to avoid the broken glass, and pulled out their drink bottles. It was a challenge searching, when they didn't know what they were looking for. Max then had another idea.

'How about we do a bit of digging, without the detector. Get down under the surface a bit and remove the top layer. Anything from Victorian times will be further down.'

'Good idea, we have two spades. Where shall we start?' Danny didn't rush to get up. They looked across the pit, which was circular, and about 4 metres in diameter, squared off a bit on one side where it backed on to the boundary for a modern woodland bungalow.

'Let's start on that edge digging down about 20 centimetres, to see what we can find. Not just metal, but anything interesting.' The boys dug. They dragged the soil to the edge of the pit with their trowels and worked tirelessly together, sweating and sighing in their hunt for something special. After about half an hour, a trench a metre wide by two metres long, lay before them. On the bank, sat a small pile of glass bottles, of varying sizes. After a break for more sustenance, they got back on their knees with trowels in hand once more.

'I've got a good feeling that we are going to find something Max,' said Danny enthusiastically. 'There has to be something here, there just *has* to.'

'Well I have just hit something very hard.' Max looked up, with eyebrows raised, trying to contain a sudden excitement he felt. 'Here Dan, come and help me dig in this area.' Max moved over as Danny joined him. The object was solid and a definite box shape, a rusting corner protruded at an angle from the soil. The boys worked at the edges, scraping away to reveal matching rusty sides. The box seemed to be quite large, but enthused by the discovery of something other than a glass bottle, the boys worked on with renewed vigour. An hour passed quickly, with the box revealing itself slowly. At last, they had cleared enough soil from the edges enabling the boys to pull the box free. They stumbled backwards together, with the box tumbling open as they fell. The box. Heavy, metal and rusty, but not locked. As the boys scrambled back to their feet, peering into the container with excitement, their joy was short lived. The box was empty. After all their efforts, there was nothing, and even worse, they had lost track of time while digging. Dinner was at 6pm, and it was now nearly 20 past.

'Oh no Dan, my mum will be cross if we are too late back. She worries.' Max sat up, looking around for the trowels and bag. 'We need to go back.'

'You are the one who worries Max,' Dan teased. 'We aren't *that* late, anyway we had to finish this dig.' Danny wasn't too despondent. He had enjoyed the digging, with and without the metal detector, and would have carried on if it hadn't been so late.

'Well help me push the box back into the hole, so that it isn't too obvious we have been digging.' Max was on his feet and leaning over the box.

As the metal box slid back into the hole, a faintly audible, tinny clunk could be heard. As if metal hit metal. Danny looked at Max.

'Did you hear that Max? It hit something hard.' Danny leant forward as if to grab the box.

'No Dan, we have to go. It was probably just a stone, or another glass bottle. Come on, we need to get back.' Max turned to climb back out of the pit, and reluctantly Danny followed.

How close had they been to a big discovery? As the light faded, the friends retraced their steps, and jogged swiftly back to the house, to face the wrath of Martha.

18
GOING BACK TO GET CHARLIE

Martha was running late with dinner, and unaware of the time, so the boys were lucky as they slipped in through the back door dropping their trowels just outside, before they entered the kitchen.

'Have you had a good afternoon boys?' Martha turned from the cooker with two plates of egg and chips held in her gloved hands. 'Go and wash your hands please, dinner is ready. Can you call Archie while you are out there - and be quick, both of you.'

The boys ate tea quickly before heading upstairs for an evening of planning. It was very clear they needed to go back to see Charlie. They discussed their next adventure as if it was just another normal day. Get up, time travel, talk to some Victorians, go home. Easy as that. But they had a Saxon soldier to find, and needed to locate whatever it was he had lost. The 'vital precious item' as Bill had put it, that would get him home. They had to get back to the cellar, and they had to go soon. The exertions of the day caught up with them, and an early night saw them both fast asleep by 9.

The following day was bright, and Danny was awake early; eager as ever to get going. They had agreed the night before that they wanted a full day if possible, and the earlier the start, the better. Danny got up and showered. He felt at ease in the Perry's home, and treated it just like his own. Back in the bedroom, Max was awake and sitting up in bed.

'Come on Max,' said Danny with gentle encouragement.

'Yeah, ok, I'm resting my body. I ache after that digging yesterday.' Max slid back down under his duvet.

'Get up and shower, lazy bones, it's 'Find a Saxon Soldier' day!' Danny laughed as he teased his friend, and Max reluctantly trundled out of the bedroom towards the bathroom.

An hour later, clean and breakfasted the boys were ready to go out. With the arrowhead securely in Max's pocket as always, they set off towards the Iron Age ring ditch, heading for the far side as they had done previously.

There were several families in the ring, enjoying the sunshine and the tree lined ditch, as so many families had done before them. A small child ran up and down the slope at the point where the boys needed to exit the ring, and enter the past, by the dishevelled privet hedge. The two boys casually hung around, trying to look inconspicuous until the families had gone past.

'Right Max, after three,' Danny counted as they ran up the sloped bank and dropped to the ground by the hedge, wriggling through expertly as before, the gap this time a little wider. As they stood up in their 19th century field, the horse was nowhere to be seen, possibly out with the carriage surmised the boys. They had a quick look about, but the coast seemed clear so they half walked, half ran across the field to the gate and jumped over. The yard was empty, but the back door was open.

'I suppose we will just have to go to the back door and hope that Molly or Charlie are there, and not the cook or the chauffeur!' Danny smiled, enjoying today's adventure even before it had begun. They approached the door and entered quietly. Suddenly the door from the kitchen into the main house flung open, and a boy, about their age appeared, shouting for the cook. He was very smartly dressed in a tweed jacket, trousers and a shirt and tie. Quite odd looking on a boy of his age, they thought. They ducked back into the door way, just in time to avoid a very difficult meeting. The door to the cellar opened, and Charlie appeared.

'Good day to you Master Albert,' said Charlie addressing the other boy, 'Cook isn't here at the moment, she is in the village buying provisions for dinner tonight.'

'Very good Charlie, I'll come back later,' said the boy they now knew as Master Albert. Albert turned and went back through the door to the main house, and Charlie closed the cellar door behind him. As he turned back to the kitchen he saw Max and Danny standing in the doorway, grinning.

'Hiya Charlie,' said Danny 'we came back! We said we would.' A broad grin crept across Charlie's face, and he went over to the boys, embracing briefly. His joy at meeting them again was evident.

'We've come to take you back to our time, Charlie,' said Max, 'we would like you to help us with the tunnels. We have to find something special and we think you can help.'

'Oh, but I can't leave. I have work to do. I will be beaten if I don't do my job.' Charlie was visibly anxious, when the door opened again and in walked Molly.

'Oh boys, you're back?' Molly unconsciously glanced back over her shoulder, but smiled her wide glowing smile.

'We are,' said Dan, Max jumping into the conversation too.

'We want to take Charlie back to our time Molly - can you cover for him while he is with us?' Max spoke keenly.

'What do you mean, cover for him? It's my afternoon off today. I really don't know Max, it's risky.'

Then without any warning, the door burst open and Master Albert returned, striding into the kitchen towards the group of friends. The children stepped back in shock.

'Ha!' Exclaimed Albert, 'I knew you had friends here, I could hear there were unfamiliar voices. I'm going to report this, unless you let me join in!' Albert stood with his hands on his hips, and grinned at them. Molly went quickly towards him, and ushering him to the large kitchen table, she suggested he sat down.

'Now Albert, don't be hasty. Let me introduce you to our new special friends. Take a seat and I'll get us all a glass of freshly made lemonade.' She pulled out a heavy kitchen chair and Albert sat down, her eyebrows raised, and staring intensely at the others her face said to do the same. Moments later, she returned to the table with a jug full of fragrant lemon drink and five glasses, where all four boys were now sitting.

'Oh, I don't know about this Molly,' Albert's forehead crumpled in puzzlement.

Albert was not a child who enjoyed his status in life. He had no friends of his own age, and no siblings. Forced to mix with adults, at formal gatherings with his parents the Lord and Lady, or isolated with just Nanny Carpenter for company, he was always feeling a bit left out. He had been known to get into mischief, and his parents had employed several tutors who had struggled to satisfy the brief given. To give the boy a rounded education in the essential subjects, whilst keeping control and discipline. No mean feat. Albert was a challenging, lively and really quite naughty boy. The tutors failed and were dismissed, only to be succeeded by a series of equally unsuccessful replacements.

They all took the lemonade offered, and drank gratefully. Albert peered over the rim of the glass as he drank. Placing the cup back on the heavy wooden table, he wiped his mouth with the back of his hand, before letting out a sigh.

'So who are you then?' he said looking from Max to Danny with a slight grin, 'and why the funny clothes?'

'Oh here we go again,' said Danny, 'I could say the same about you.' The boys stared at one another, but in a friendly, amused way. Trying to suss each other out.

'Ok, well here's the deal,' said Danny finally. 'My name is Danny, and this is my friend Max. If you like you can join us on a..' Danny paused, 'let me see; a little adventure. However, you must let Charlie come too. We need Charlie as part of our plan.'

Max looked across at Danny, wondering what was going to come out of his mouth next. He certainly wasn't aware of any plan.

Danny went on. 'We have to save a Saxon soldier, and in addition, we have the challenge of finding something he has lost, so that he can be returned to his own time. So how about it? Are you in?' At this, Albert's face dropped, and the colour drained from his cheeks. Molly stood up, concerned at the visible change to her young Master.

'Come now boys, no more talk of this nonsense. Young Albert are you feeling quite alright?' Molly gathered the glasses and the boys pushed back from the table.

'I..er.. am very busy actually,' stuttered Albert, still looking peaky, 'I've just remembered I do have some work my tutor gave me to do today.' He backed away, towards the door. 'Don't worry, I won't tell on you,' were his final mutterings as he made his exit.

The remaining four looked at each other in bewilderment. Was it something that Danny had said, which scared young Albert off? It seemed a very odd reaction.

'So,' Max spoke to Charlie with authority, 'are you coming back with us now, or not?' Charlie looked at Molly. He wanted an adventure, although he didn't really understand what the boys were offering, he really did like the idea of visiting someone else's home.

'Oh, go on then Charlie,' said Molly 'I'll cover for you, but try not to be too long. We aren't expecting anyone today, and Albert won't be back down now, I am sure. He seems well and truly frightened off by something. Funny lad. Off you scoot now, before I change my mind.'

The three boys needed no further encouragement, and with a slight skip in their steps, they headed out of the back door, towards the 21st century.

19
ALBERT FINDS OSWULF

Albert took himself straight up to his room. He felt out of sorts, and didn't know what to do about it. What was this feeling? Guilt perhaps? It was unlike anything he had felt before. Had he reacted rather impulsively, under the circumstances, he thought? He sat on his bed to consider what he should do next. Pouring himself a glass of water from the jug on his dressing table, he then slumped back. He really had got himself into a pickle this time. Perhaps the funny looking boys would be his way out of it. A new-found guilt over his secret, was starting to eat into him, and he knew he had to tell someone. Poor Molly and Cook were obeying his orders to leave food outside the big door. They would be very disappointed with him if they knew the truth.

Albert started to think through the day in question, going over the series of events in his mind.

It had been a bright crisp March morning; the winter was still hanging on, with just glimmers of spring appearing in the newly budding trees, and the bright yellow and lilac carpet of crocus' and aconites, and just a few white snowdrops peeking through. Albert always rose early. He liked to walk around the garden grounds, to see what he could find, often taking the gardener's tools if they took his fancy. He hadn't been caught yet, and why should the gardener have things to dig and cut; prune and rake, when he had nothing in his life but fine clothes and leather-bound books for company? On that spring morning, he had found Oswulf, during his walk, huddled behind the gardener's shed, curled up for warmth. Albert had thought he was a dirty down and out tramp. A worthless human being who had no value to society; the lowest class of human, is how he saw him.

Looking back, his conscience pricked at what he did next. A shiver ran down his spine. It had been the glint of a shiny gem, and silver blade, which led to the action he took next. Mindless, thoughtless and out of character for the son of an upstanding family such as the Greyfords. Albert had a greed for possessions, a greed for all things of value. This body; the man; started to uncurl as Albert approached. His footsteps audible through the frosty undergrowth.

Slightly panicked, Albert had moved quickly. Impulsively he had lunged towards the sword, grasped it by its ornate handle, and had then swung it above his head. The cowering man had looked up, fear filling his hooded eyes. He had muttered something unrecognisable to Albert, a whimper of sorts, and he'd lifted his hands as if to protect his head. Albert had gestured to him, to stand up, and holding the sword horizontally, had pointed it straight at the man's chest. As he did so, the man had stood up with his hands still over his head. Submissive. That was when Albert noticed the man's attire. A soldier stood before him, unusual in his dress, but definitely a soldier. Albert had looked around, and with no one else in sight, had roughly herded the poor man towards the house, and straight down the outer tower which lead to the cellar tunnels. There, he pushed along the dark tunnel to a cell, with a heavy door. Using the solid handle of the magnificent sword, he pushed the soldier roughly, catching the back of his head quite heavily. He closed the door, ensuring the latch clunked firmly shut.

In his haste to hide the sword, he had returned to the vegetable garden, with it wrapped tightly in one of his old heavy cotton nightshirts, and buried it in a pile of tree and shrub cuttings, that had been mounting for quite a while by the gardener's shed. His intention had been to return after dark and retrieve the sword. But disaster. Returning to the spot three days later, as the light was dimming, he discovered that the whole pile of brash and vegetation had vanished, including the prized sword. Albert had felt a sick feeling in his stomach, then an anger welled inside him. Irrationally he had blamed the stranger for the loss of this treasure, vowing to punish him.

Even as he thought back, he couldn't really explain why he had done it. The poor defenceless man had been very frightened. Now so much time had passed, with the man living alone in the cellar, he didn't really know what to do next.

Over time his anger had subsided, he had to face his secret head on. A man in his cellar. A prisoner. He regretted his actions, and now wanted more than anything to turn the clock back. He knew he had to set the man free, but he needed help to do it. These strange boys seemed to be looking for a soldier. It seemed quite likely that this was the man they were looking for. It might be his opportunity to put things right. It was time to confess and Charlie would be his first port of call.

20
THE CELLAR TUNNEL

'After the count of three drop down on your belly, and wriggle through that gap in the hedge.' Max's instructions were very clear to the other two boys. 'All together now. One, two, three.' They were through the hedge in no time, up on their feet and half running, half stumbling down the steep bank of the ditch, to the flat area at its foot. Then turning briskly homeward, all three boys skipped happily back along the ring ditch, through the Yew Tree Circle and home. As they entered the garden, careful with the cranky gate, Max scurried forwards to the cellar door. Situated at the back of the cottage, it was not overlooked by any windows, apart from a tiny one in the bathroom upstairs. Once he was sure the way was clear, Max beckoned to the other two, then opened the cellar door. The boys descended the old stone steps, closing the door behind them. Charlie was the first to speak, as they sank their bottoms onto the lowest step to catch their breath.

'It's old Mr Rowbottom's house, this one. The gardener,' he looked up at Max a little anxiously.

'It isn't Mr Rowbottom's house, Charlie, it's my house now. We are in the year 2018, not 1861 anymore.'

Max laughed. Poor Charlie didn't understand what Max was saying to him. The light in the cellar was dim. Charlie wasn't sure if he was enjoying the adventure or not, but as he had escaped duties, even for a short while, he decided he had to make the most of the freedom.

'So, what are we here for?' said Charlie. 'What is it you need me in particular to help you with?' Charlie looked from Max to Danny and back again.

'You know about the tunnels, Charlie, don't you?' Danny wanted to get down to the nitty gritty.

'You mean the one from here to the Manor House?' Charlie started to get up, but room at the foot of the cellar steps was cramped.

'I knew it!' Max squealed and got up at the same time, jostling with the other two boys for space. 'We have been trying to move the shelved area just under here,' he pointed to the gap where they had previously shone their torches. 'Grab the torch Dan, it is up on that hook behind your head. Just up the steps a bit.' Danny turned and found the torch quickly, and they huddled together to shine a beam of light under the shelving. 'See,' continued Max, 'there is a space under there, but boarding in front of it, which almost seals the tunnel.'

Charlie was confused once more. He had only ever known a tunnel, but seeing it boarded up like this threw him.

'What is this all doing here, how do you use the tunnel with that in the way?' Charlie crouched down on his knees, then down on his belly he edged forwards.

'Be careful Charlie, you will get filthy dirty down there.' Said Danny, thoughtlessly.

'I think it's a bit late for that,' replied Charlie in a joking manner. 'Pass me the torch you have there, and I will go under to see what is there.' His voice echoed as he wriggled through, torch in hand. 'Yes, the tunnel is just the same, we can get through here.' Charlie reappeared with a dusty look of satisfaction on his grinning face. Danny looked across at his friend, and smiling they pulled Charlie to his feet.

'Do you know what Max?' said Danny 'I think we need to talk to Master Albert again. Come on boys, it's still early. Next stop 1861. Again!'

21
FINDING ALBERT

The three boys climbed the crumbling cellar stairs, which brought them back out into the daylight. The adventure was increasing pace, and the boys were driven on by excitement and adrenaline, to find a solution to the puzzle Bill had set them.

The only sure way to return to the exact point in 1861, where they had left the 19th century earlier that day, was to go back using the arrowhead and the Iron Age ring ditch. It was only 10 o'clock, so plenty of time for more adventure. They left the torch just inside the cellar entrance, and took a different path out of the garden, through George's yard. Here they had to wind their way through tractors, other big work tools and heavy vehicles all crammed together. As they carefully picked their way through, Charlie was in awe, and hung back as he stared first at the tractor, and then the Land Rover. There was nothing like it in his world. He reached up to grab the handle of the Land Rover, and, pulling himself up onto the step he peered in to the cab. The closest this Victorian boy came to transport was old Henry and the horse and carriage. Of course, apart from the day he was brought to the family, the carriage was only ever used by the Lord and Lady. He jumped down, and caught up with the other two boys and they left the yard, choosing the main track to take them back to the ring.

'We need to see if Albert is feeling any better,' said Danny, keen to push on with their plan. 'He was a bit odd, and I noticed it was after we mentioned the soldier. Did anyone else think the same?' Danny looked from one boy to the other. Their faces both looked blank, and Max shook his head. Danny seemed surprised. 'Really? But as soon as we invited him to help us find the Saxon soldier, he went quiet and, well, just a bit odd.'

'I suppose,' said Max in feeble agreement.

'Molly will be there. We can tell her we've come back to make friends with Albert, and then get to speak with him again. We need him in on this. I am sure he knows something.' Danny was walking faster as he spoke, and the other two boys had to jog almost to keep up.

There were still people in the park, enjoying the summer holidays, but as they approached the right spot, the coast was clear for a quick entrance to the past. On the count of three, as before, the boys wriggled under the hedge.

The plan was now quite clear in the minds of Danny and Max. Charlie would tag along. They had to find and make amends with Albert. Then would come the tricky bit; asking him again about the soldier. They would also need somewhere out of sight to get together. They couldn't risk getting caught by Reynolds, Henry or Cook, and especially Lord and Lady Greyford. There really was quite a lot to do, and still a soldier and the mystery item to find.

Whatever that was. Perhaps they were hoping for too much. Happy endings only happened in story books they thought. Didn't they?

After crossing the paddock, the three adventurers strode towards the kitchen door, keeping an eye out for any adults and horses. With no one around outside, it was just the cook they needed to get past. They knew she had been shopping earlier in the day, for a special Ball that was being held in the Manor House that evening. They decided the safest thing was to send Charlie in first then follow when the coast was clear.

'Good morning again Charlie, that was a very short break out with your new friends,' Molly was the only one in the kitchen, and gave Charlie her usual friendly smile as he entered the room.

'Oh really? Well we changed our plans, and now we are back. Max and Danny too. They are outside, but I'm going to bring them in as Cook isn't here,' Charlie was growing in confidence, and Molly noticed this in her young friend.

'You are taking a chance, Charlie, but ok, bring them in,' said Molly, as Charlie quickly stepped back outside and beckoned to his friends.

'Hiya Molls,' was Danny's cheeky greeting to Molly, who gave him a friendly frown. 'We're back again. We want to see Albert, as soon as possible.' Molly's frown became sterner.

'Is that wise, do you think? He wasn't quite himself just a short while ago, when you met for the first time.' Molly was cut short by Danny, who walked over to the door leading into the main house, and opened it.

'Oh, he'll be fine,' he said rashly, 'just lead the way Charlie, to Albert's room.' Max followed his confident friend, and Charlie had no choice but to go with him, edging past him in the corridor, in order to lead the way. Molly looked on, dumbstruck, but said nothing more. It was then Charlie's turn to take charge, and issue some clear instructions. To Danny more than Max, being the hot head, determined to push ahead.

'Slow down Danny, and quieten down too.' Charlie whispered loudly, but firmly, putting his finger to his lips in a 'be quiet' gesture. 'Cook isn't back yet from the village, and the Lord and Lady are not in either. I will lead the way up to Master Albert's room, but you must be quiet. I don't want to be caught.' The boys nodded, and followed Charlie up the wide, grand carpeted staircase. Excited, knowing they were at last one step closer to finding their missing soldier.

22
TALKING TO ALBERT

Albert was leaning back on his bed when he thought he heard a faint tap at his door. There it was again, a little louder this time. He propped himself up on his elbows.

'Please enter,' said Albert hesitantly. As the door slowly opened, he rose to his feet to greet the three boys. Surprise at his unexpected visitors was clearly etched on Albert's face. Charlie smiled at his Master reassuringly.

'Good day Master Albert, I am sorry to disturb you, but my, er..' he stumbled over his words, unsure of exactly how to describe his relationship with Max and Danny. 'My friends here, they are very keen to speak to you again. *Very* keen. I hope you don't mind?' Charlie sighed. Albert, by this time, had moved towards the small group of boys, stood in the doorway. His room was plush with ornate fittings. A beautiful patterned rug on the floor and long red velvet drapes at the window. Signs of the wealth he enjoyed; so different to Charlie's own room, up in the attic.

'I..umm,' it was now Albert's turn to hesitate as he too stuttered his reply, trying hard to choose the right words to respond, but not really knowing what to say. 'Er.., I mean, please do come in, and close the door. Please. All of you.'

The three boys shuffled in, and Max closed the door behind him. Charlie was careful to stay in front, to exert some control over the boys. He was sure that Danny in particular, would be keen to explore. This was his Master's room, and normally out of bounds, unless by special invitation. He didn't want to be seen to take advantage.

'Wow,' said Danny, gazing up at the lavish wall hangings, and extravagant four-poster bed. It really was beyond anything he had ever seen in his 21st century life. 'This is amazing Albert. Cool. Just cool.'

'Thank you, Danny,' Albert replied, 'you're funny.' Albert smiled. Danny's friendly confidence had broken the ice. 'Come right in and sit down here.' Albert pointed to a large leather Chesterfield sofa, in front of the big bay window. Danny was there like a shot.

'Albert, you have a great view from your room. I can just see the old potting shed, and a bit beyond.' Danny leant forwards as the other boys all took a seat. Max glanced out, thinking he was glad it didn't overlook the field with the horse and stables. That would be tricky. There was a short silence. Max and Danny looked at one another; one of them had to broach the subject. Max took a deep breath.

'Well it's like this Albert, you remember when we met you this morning, Danny mentioned that we are looking for someone?' Max was putting off saying the words '*Saxon soldier*' but he knew he could only skirt around the subject for so long, before Danny would jump in. Albert nodded but said nothing. 'Good. And do you remember that the person we are looking for, the *man* we are looking for, is a soldier, who needs our help?'

'Yes, yes, yes,' exploded Albert, his cry of the affirmative took everyone by surprise. He stood up, and walked to the window. Running his hand through his curly fair hair, his face contorted with anguish. 'Yes' he said again. 'I know about the soldier. I confess. I've been bad and I feel terrible. I need your help more than you need mine. I need to free him and make things right again.' Albert's speech was rambling and quickening. The boys sat in silence, mouths gaping and eyes wide. It was more than they had ever expected. It was Danny's turn to speak.

'I knew you knew something. I just knew it!' with glee Danny grinned at the less than happy face of Master Albert. 'So. Where is he?' Impatient as ever, Danny wanted answers.

'I need to explain,' said Albert, sitting back down next to Charlie, and breathing a heavy sigh, released at last of his burdensome secret. With the three boys looking on, Albert gave a detailed explanation of what had happened on the morning he had stumbled unexpectedly upon Oswulf, and his life in the intervening months. The boys were spell bound. Silently allowing Albert to unburden himself of his terrible secret. When he was finished they all relaxed back into the sofa, stunned at the news. Danny had been sure Albert knew something, but never in his wildest dreams had he reckoned on kidnap.

'The tunnel.' Max had a light bulb moment. 'Danny, do you remember that day we were stuck for ages in the cellar, and we walked along the tunnel to a dead end? We heard voices behind the big oak door that had no handle. Do you remember?'

'Yes Max, I remember, and the voice we heard,' Danny looked towards Albert 'it was your voice, wasn't it Albert?' Albert nodded and Danny stood up. 'We need to plan what we do next. Is everyone in agreement?' Danny looked to Max who nodded.

'But Dan, aren't you forgetting something?' Max looked up at his best friend. 'The missing item. We still need to find out what this is. Do you think it could be his sword? Albert has told us that it disappeared. He went back and it wasn't there. That is certainly something special, that he can't leave without. What does everyone think?' There were nods all round from the other boys. So, the soldier had a precious sword, now missing, which they still had to locate.

'Ha,' said Danny with a satisfied grin on his face, 'I have a plan which might help with that too. Are you all ready to hear my plan?' The boys nodded again. Danny had everyone's attention. That was just the way he liked it.

23
MAKING MORE PLANS

'Ok, my plan is this. It may need refining – actually I am still formulating it in my mind but..'

'Just tell us what you are thinking Dan, and then *we* can decide,' cut in Max, getting a little impatient with his friend, 'we can't stay in Albert's room all day, or we are sure to get caught by someone.' Max stood up and walked to the window. Danny continued.

'Alright Max, well as I was saying, my first idea about finding the sword is to ask the gardener what he does with his garden rubbish pile.'

'Excellent idea boy,' Master Albert had renewed energy now his secret was shared, and was keen to get on with releasing the man. 'The gardener, old Mr Rowbottom, lives in the cottage on the far side of the estate, on the outside of the wall, over the Iron Age ring ditch.' At the mention of travelling so far, and especially out of the protection of the ring, Max and Danny looked anxiously at one another. Charlie, who had been silent until now, spoke up.

'You know Max; the house you took me to. The one you called your house. It's easy, we can get there through the tunnel.' Charlie had offered the perfect solution, to which Max smiled and nodded.

The tunnel ran from the big house, in many directions, one of which went straight to Max's cottage, which in 1861 had been the residence of the gardener and his family. There were several entrances on the estate, but as a servant, Charlie was wise to all of them. The entrance he had in mind, was near to the gate, and was used to receive deliveries of coal, food and wine. Charlie used it often. Albert looked puzzled.

'What do you mean Charlie, calling Stewards Cottage 'Max's house'? Max clearly does not live there; old Mr Rowbottom and his family live there, and have done for many years. You know that.' Albert needed the time travelling explained, but even Charlie hadn't worked that one out, and now really wasn't the time. In fact, both Max and Danny were wondering themselves about the time travelling, and what would happen if they went down the tunnel, and then crossed the ring underneath. Could they possibly travel outside the ring, and still stay in Victorian Britain? They surmised that the only way to find out was to try it.

'We'll explain later, Albert,' said Danny, and winked to Charlie.

'Ok,' said Danny 'the plan is coming together in my mind now. We just need to decide when we are going to go for it. When is a good time to creep about without getting caught?'

'I know,' said Albert, raising his hand in an excited gesture, 'this evening my parents are hosting a dance in the grand ballroom, so all the garden staff will be dismissed early. Only the Head Butler and his footmen will be working.' Albert was smiling now. He was happy to be contributing to the plan.

'But doesn't that mean Charlie will be needed?' said Max, concerned.

'Of course not, that's absurd,' chastised Albert, 'the boy will most definitely have to stay out of sight. That is what the tunnels are for. The servants use them to hide in, if they see a family member. My parents are very particular. They do not like to see servants when they are at home.' Albert still had a superior tone to his voice. Charlie stood up and turned to the group, seated and standing.

'It is time boys,' he was short, but spoke with urgency, 'I must take you to the tower. There I will leave you until late afternoon. I still have chores to do, but once the way is clear for us, Albert and I will join you and then we can follow the tunnel that leads to your…er, I mean to Mr Rowbottom's home.'

'Here we go again,' said Max 'this is like déjà vu.'

'I'm sorry Max, I don't understand,' said Charlie, walking towards the door. The boys followed him.

'Oh, don't worry about it, I was just thinking about the last time we got shoved in your smelly cellar,' Max was disgruntled, but far less anxious than on his earlier adventures.

'Just think,' said Danny 'this time we are a step closer to solving this mystery. What harm can another few hours in a cold damp cellar do?' Danny laughed. As they opened the bedroom door, Charlie held his finger to his lips, indicating silence was required. Albert waved and nodded to Charlie who took the lead, down the main stairs, and then to the left down a narrow plainly decorated corridor. They reached a big, solid outside door they hadn't seen before. Charlie heaved it open.

'Now Max and Danny, can you see on the other side of the courtyard, that square bricked up area?' Charlie was pointing to a space between the perimeter wall which circled his home, and the entrance road by which all deliveries were made. At the junction of these, there was indeed a low wall, with grass so high it almost covered the three-brick high structure. The two boys nodded.

'There are steps which lead down to the cellar. There is a door, but it has no lock. Go down there, and wait for us. Stay hidden. I will bring Master Albert, and we will join you very soon.' Charlie seemed very self-assured all of a sudden. The shy boy they had met originally, was gaining confidence daily. He seemed to have cottoned on to the plan, and was taking charge of this small part. He was the one who knew the tunnel system, and that made him feel important.

Max and Danny made a dash for the cellar entrance. A short sprint for two fit boys, and they were down the steps in an instant. Once Charlie saw their heads disappear, he closed the house door and turned back down the corridor to find Molly. He would still need a bit of cover from her later on, depending on how long they were out. It was a bit of luck about the Greyford's Ball though. That would give them lots of time and everyone would be distracted! He was already looking forward to another exciting adventure with his two new friends, and was it possible, that the only other boy in the household, Master Albert, was warming to him also? It really would be nice to have a friend of his own age. His life was improving every day!

24
MR ROWBOTTOM

The minutes turned to hours for Danny and Max waiting, just inside the entrance to the tunnel. There was an oil lamp fixed to a shelf, which was already lit when they entered, but being the main entrance for deliveries, they supposed that was normal. Further on into the tunnel, they could just make out the flicker of another light. They sat on the bottom step playing I spy, rock, paper, scissors and any other game they could think of. Quietly together they had taken it in turns to recite vegetables, animals, and boy's names for each of the letters of the alphabet. They'd run out of games, and Max was now kicking his heels into a bit of soft ground in boredom, but Danny was still upbeat.

'What I didn't say while we were all together Max, was that I have been thinking about something. Something to do with the time travel and the arrowhead,' at this Max looked up.

'What about it?' he said.

'Well, you remember the time we saw the Romans? The very first time we time travelled, but we didn't know it?' Max nodded. 'You had the arrowhead in your pocket, so we time travelled. Then when we took your dad back, you didn't have the arrowhead, and we didn't time travel.'

'Yes Danny, of course I know that, but what is your point?' Getting tired, and hungry, Max's impatience was showing.

'Well, we need to travel down the tunnel, and stay in the same year; in Victorian time. We need to find Mr Rowbottom. If you have the arrowhead in your pocket, we will travel back to some unknown time, or forward even, as soon as we cross the ring border. That's what Bill said.'

Danny was right. They couldn't chance ending up in another random time zone. This mission to find Mr Rowbottom, and hopefully the whereabouts of the sword was too important. Max sat up straight.

'You have got a point Dan.' He pulled the arrowhead, wrapped in his hanky, out of his pocket. 'I'll put it up here behind the oil lamp. We can collect it on our way back out.' As Max wedged the arrowhead firmly behind the fixed oil lamp, there was the sound of footsteps on the steps outside, and before they were able to even think about hiding, Charlie and then Albert appeared through the door, both smiling.

'Oh boy,' loudly sighed Albert as he slumped to the floor, breathing heavily from the short run. The boy was a little overweight, and not at all fit. His clothes were not really suited to running either, but both Max and Danny were relieved to see them.

'Well done lads,' said Danny, patting Charlie on the back, 'now let's get going!'

Once Albert had caught his breath, it was Charlie's job to lead the way. The tunnel was dark, apart from the glimmer of the oil lamps. Thick cobwebs attached themselves to the boys' shoulders, as they brushed through the tunnel. As they approached the next lamp, they could see it wasn't fixed to the wall, and Charlie took it by the handle, to guide their way. There were unlit candles periodically placed along the wall. When the tunnel was in full use, these were lit, explained Charlie to the others. After a short walk, the tunnel forked. Albert seemed to know where they were.

'Not that way, Charlie' he said pointing to the left. 'That takes us to the dead end, to the cell where the soldier is being kept.' Albert's voice became quieter with shame. Charlie pushed on.

'That's correct Master Albert, we need to take the right-hand tunnel here, and then, just about here…' Charlie stopped, and lifted the lamp to the wall, where they could see a door, with a handle this time. Charlie pulled open the door. 'This tunnel will take us straight to Mr Rowbottom's cellar.'

In unison there was a sharp intake of breath from Max and Danny. Momentarily they hesitated, then first Danny and then Max, followed by Albert, went through the doorway after Charlie.

This tunnel was narrower, and more stale smelling than the first one. It didn't feel very used. The ground was stony earth, and the walls were damp. Cobwebs were huge, spanning the width of the tunnel. Charlie ducked down to avoid them. It was difficult to see with the light up in front, and they stumbled to keep together, trying hard not to trip each other up. Danny squealed as he met a cobweb full in the face.

'Oh yuck,' he said as he pawed at his face to remove the stickiness, but luckily he didn't have a spider phobia, and the boys pushed on. It was a long walk, and difficult to guess where they were in relation to the park and estate above them. It was hard to imagine they were under the ground, and Max tried to push the thought from his mind. He had to be brave and face his fears.

It was cold. Colder than when they had just been in the cellar, and the small group hurried along, ignoring the occasional scuffle at their feet as a lone rat raced past them, disturbed by their presence. Eventually, Charlie stopped and held up the lamp.

'We are here,' he whispered loudly.

'Cool!' was Danny's reply to loud shushing from the other boys.

'What now?' said Max.

'I think I take over from here,' said Albert pushing forwards. 'I know Mr Rowbottom, we get on quite well I think. Considering.'

'Considering what?' said Danny.

'Considering he is a servant, you know, not of my class.' Albert spoke in seriousness; with the superior tone he just couldn't help.

'Go on then,' said Charlie, and held out the lamp, as Albert squeezed through from the back of the group.

As the boys crept forwards, they emerged out of the tunnel, into a familiar space. The cellar, shelved and stocked with wine was no different to the one in Max's current day version of the house, apart from the fact that the entrance to the tunnel was open. Albert climbed the stone staircase and gently opened the door to the outside. He paused and looked about. The other boys joined him.

'Let's try his vegetable garden. I think that is where we will find Mr Rowbottom,' said Albert, 'come on out, quickly, and then I'll close the door.' It was Max's turn to look around in awe at the beautiful old building, manicured gardens and what looked like a brand new glass greenhouse in the corner. This garden had been neglected greatly since Victorian times, and Max considered how sad that was. Mr Rowbottom clearly took great pride in his gardens, at work on the estate, and here in his own home. He jogged to catch the other boys, who were heading towards the greenhouse.

Sure enough, a figure, clothed in a heavy, grey oversized waistcoat, and baggy trousers, was bent over his garden fork, in the centre of a lush green vegetable patch. He didn't notice the boys approach, so Albert cleared his throat loudly.

'Excuse me Mr Rowbottom,' Albert paused, as Mr Rowbottom looked up, and turned. 'Ah Mr Rowbottom, what a lovely day it is, and how fine your garden is looking today.' Albert was very good at getting people on side.

'Young Master Albert, how do you do on this fine day?' Mr Rowbottom lifted his cap to his Master and began to pick his way along the wooden boards protecting the vegetable garden, towards the small group. 'And I see you have friends with you, and, is that young Charlie from the big house?' Charlie nodded. He decided to leave the explanations to Albert.

'Yes, that's right, Charlie and two of our local friends. We have made a special,' he winked back at the boys, 'a very special trip out to see you today. We want to ask you a question, if we may?'

'Ah, well I can't promise I will be able to answer, but fire away young man, fire away and I'll see what I can do.'
At that point, Albert thought about the question he was about to ask. Would Mr Rowbottom wonder why they wanted an old pile of brush, and garden waste? He decided he just had to ask the question.

'Well, we were wondering where you move all your garden waste to, when the pile by the shed gets too big?' They all looked to the old man, holding their breath waiting for his response.

'Oh that's an easy question, Albert, of course it all goes to the pit, along with all the other household waste. Smelly old place. You don't want to be going around there.' His voice was dismissive. 'Was that it?'

'Yes Mr Rowbottom, thank you,' said Danny, already with a knowing twinkle in his eye. He nodded at the blank expression on his friend's faces. 'Thank you, we must go now.' Danny pulled at the sleeves of Max and Charlie, and began to walk away.

'That was a brief visit, but I'm glad I could help.' He watched as the boys hurried back towards the cellar entrance. 'So what do you need to know that for?' Was a question that was left hanging in the air, as by this time, the boys had all disappeared back into the tunnel, intent on finding the special sword as soon as they possibly could.

25
FINDING THE SWORD

Before emerging back out into the fresh air, after retracing their steps through the tunnel, Max surreptitiously retrieved his arrowhead from its hiding place. Charlie replaced the oil lamp and the boys edged the door open to let some light in.

'Sit down here,' ordered Danny. He was excited, and clearly had an idea. Danny always had an idea. They did as they were told, and sat. 'The pit. The gardener said the pit.' Danny was glowing with excitement 'Max, it's where we went to dig. Your dad calls it the Victorian pit. It was full of rubbish, broken bottles, plates, and all manner of other things. Remember that big box Max?'

'How can I forget, Danny, it took ages to get it out – and then it was empty.' Max still didn't understand where this was going.

'So, have you forgotten that we ran out of time? That it was so late we had to return for tea and that just as we pushed the box back, there was a tinny thud when it fell back into its hole,' Danny continued, 'have you forgotten all that Max?' There was a slow recognition of something, creeping across Max's face. He nodded.

'You might have something there Danny,' Max started to grin, 'you actually might have solved it Dan.' His voice rose in pitch and tempo. 'We need to go. We need to get back home.' Max got up.

'What, all of us?' said Albert, hopefully.

'I don't think so. Not this time, Bertie,' said Danny cheekily 'we can do this, the two of us, and then come back to find you, as soon as we have the sword.' Optimistic words from Danny. He really was sure this time. How close were they when they had dug in the Victorian pit the first time? It seemed as if they were about to find out.

The boys left the safety of the tunnel entrance and ran back across the courtyard to the back door, and all four of them ducked inside. The house was being prepared for the ball, and so it was time for the small group to say their goodbyes. Danny and Max couldn't risk being seen inside the house again, so it was agreed that the safest thing was for them go back out through the door they had just entered, and edge around the outside of the house, keeping close, until they turned the corner. From there, the paddock was in clear view and it was a short dash across the courtyard, and over the fence, which they now had down to a tee. The horse was on the far side of the paddock, so they half walked, half skipped the short distance to the place in the hedge where they had entered. After three, they dropped to their bellies and were back in the 21st Century.

At home, they hadn't been missed. The hands on the kitchen clock had hardly moved, although time hadn't stood still for the boys. They felt exhausted from their morning adventure, which had actually turned into a whole day in their Victorian world. It was time to eat, rest a bit, and make their next plan. Martha was preparing some lunch for George. Jess was sitting in her high chair feeding herself Marmite finger sandwiches, although there seemed to be far more Marmite on her face and the tray, than anywhere else.

'Hello boys' said Martha brightly 'are you feeling peckish after your fun in the park?' Innocently underestimating the fun these boys were having in this magical park, the boys couldn't help smiling at each other.

'Please mum, we'd murder a sandwich.'

'Yes, please Mrs Perry, I'm starving.' Danny still oozed confidence in the presence of his friend's parents.

'Have a seat at the kitchen table, and I'll see what I can rustle up.' She smiled, and winked at Danny.

After the boys had eaten a big pile of sandwiches and drunk a glass of milk each, they took themselves up to Max's room to discuss the next step. It was clear to them that they had to make another trip to the Victorian pit. They really didn't want to leave it too long, so after an hour or so chilling out in the bedroom, they decided it was time.

Their plan was to pick up the trowels from the porch, and an old hessian sack from the shed. They would need something long to hide the sword. With these all to hand, they set back out through the garden gate and along the footpath past the orchard. All the routes were familiar to the boys now, and in no time they were by the cattle field.

'Remember about the electric fence,' Max reminded his friend, but Danny didn't need telling. At the end of the field boundary, they climbed over the gate, which separated the park from the ditch area.

'We are back!' said Max, with a sigh. 'This is it. It has to be it!' Max grinned. Together, they half ran, half stumbled down into the pit, crossing to the area where they had dug previously. It was very evident that the soil was disturbed, and the corner of the box was still poking up. Some soil had fallen back into the hole, but this time, extracting the box was easy, and with two of them pulling, it came out in seconds. The box was pushed to one side, instantly forgotten.

'Ok,' said Danny 'shall I lay on my belly and dig down at the bottom? Whatever we heard clunk last time, will be very close to the surface.' Max agreed.

'Do it carefully, like they do on Time Team,' concerned that digging hard might damage anything that was there, Danny began to scrape at the soil in the area that had been underneath the box. A lump to the right began to emerge. It was covered in material, or the remains of material that had started to break down under the soil. Danny scraped further.

'Help me, Max, get down on your belly. There's room for both of us.' Max joined his friend and they frantically dug in the area of the lump. As the hole around it grew, they were able to make out the shape. In silence they dug faster, and more furiously, unable to speak, their pent-up excitement tangible.

143

'Max, I'm going to wiggle it a bit, to see if it will slide out,'
Danny didn't want to break their find, but as it was completely
encased in several layers of something resembling heavy cloth, they
needed to release it, to see if it definitely was the missing sword.
Max nodded, as Danny took hold of the protruding stick shaped
treasure and gently rocked it forwards, then back again.

'It's moving Max,' Danny's whisper was almost silent as he
held his breath, and manoeuvred it gently from side to side. 'I think
if you can get your two hands around it, near the bottom of the hole
we've made, and I do the same at the top, we can gently, gently…'
he spoke as they lifted together, a piece of metal that had possibly
been buried for 150 years. 'Gently lift it from its….that's it, Max.'
Danny grinned a muddy faced grin, to his best friend, and together
they lifted it from its final resting place, out into the open. Turning
onto their backs and somehow sitting up, they laid it onto their
outstretched legs. Now to unravel the find, and perhaps the mystery?

26
THE SWORD AND BILL

'I'm almost too scared to,' gasped Max, cheeks puffed as he held his breath, 'only almost though. Let's do it. Let's try and unwrap it here across our legs.' Still seated at the edge of their hole, at the bottom of a giant rubbish tip, the boys were a strange sight, but they didn't care what anyone thought, they were on the brink of a momentous discovery. The object was certainly very solid, and it didn't feel broken or crumbling. Slowly, glancing at each other for reassurance, they took hold of the open edge of the greying cloth, and started to roll it. To begin with, the cloth broke off in small damp pieces, the ground and the years had worked to break down the particles, as a rubbish tip does over time. As they rolled, the cloth was more intact, until it even became quite dry and the deterioration of the item less marked. A sleeve, with a tight cuff, flopped out as they unravelled slowly; evidence that the item had been wrapped carefully in a piece of clothing. And then the shape was clear, and both boys stopped.

'You have the handle end Max,' said Danny. He could feel the slim flat shape of a blade across his lap. 'Just a couple more turns, and I think it will be completely revealed.' Slowly they turned once, twice more. The tip of the sword, tarnished, but clearly of a valuable metal, edged out into the light, followed on the final turn by the beautiful ornate handle. 'Turn it over Max, is the ruby there?' Anxious to see that it was still complete, Danny urged his friend.

Max lifted the sword by its handle, and turned it over. There in the dappled shade, shone a ruby, blood red, almost glowing. It looked as fresh as the day it was cut. The boys sat in silence, quite unable to take in the whole experience. They gazed down at their laps, where the sword now lay, undressed.

'Right Dan,' Max was the first to speak 'let's get it into the sack. I'll hold it by the handle, while you stand up, then you can take it from me.' The boys manoeuvred themselves to standing, then carefully lowered the sword down into their sack. With very little communication between them, they gathered the trowel and sack together. Danny pushed the box back into the hole, and gently kicked some of last year's autumn leaf fall over the disturbed area. Then they climbed, extra carefully, up the side of the pit bank back out into the open. They climbed over the fence, and as they turned to follow the electric fence line back home, they were confronted with a friendly face.

'Boys, my, my, you boys,' sighed Bill, a big happy smile filling his face, 'I never doubted you. You are going great guns. Just one more hurdle for you now. Find our man, and reunite him with that magnificent sword, and I can take him home.' Bill was shaking his head, in a positive gesture, almost of disbelief that they had found the treasure. There was no going back, and fired with enthusiasm, the boys found their voices.

'We just knew it had to be there, Bill,' said Max hurriedly, 'we just knew it.'

'Yeah, we would have found it the first time, if we hadn't been late for tea,' said Danny, keen to impress. Bill was still smiling, he crossed in front of them, and turned as if to go back to the pit, he waved a brief farewell.

'I'll see you both anon, and no doubt your new friends,' he paused. 'And of course, Oswulf too.'

'Oswulf?' said the boys in unison, looking at each other briefly, and when they turned back to Bill, he had vanished. Into the pit, or the field, or the hedge. Who knows, but he had vanished as he had done in the past. Shrugging their shoulders, the boys hurried along the field edge, careful of the wire, and quickened their pace once on the main track back to the cottage.

'So where are we going to put the sword when we get back to yours?' said Danny. They were half jogging now, in their anxiety to get the sword back without being seen.

'I think the cellar is the best place,' said Max 'and I've been thinking about the next phase of our adventure too.'

'Go on,' said Danny intrigued.

'To get back to Albert, Charlie and er..Oswulf, we know we need to enter the ring in the same place, but we can't take the sword out, and try to wriggle under the hedge with it, in broad day light, so I was thinking we could place it down in the tunnel, from our end.'

'You mean the blocked-up tunnel from the cellar at your house?'

'Yes, I do, it's only the entrance to it, that is blocked. We saw the hole under the shelves, we go through with the sword, and leave it at the far end of the tunnel. No one is using that tunnel. We could tell that when we went through it this morning. We leave the sword there, and collect it from the other end, in Victorian time.'

'Genius!' exclaimed Danny, slapping his best friend firmly on the back 'that really is a genius idea, mate. When?' Danny's excitement was rising once more, but Max couldn't face more adventures that day.

'Tomorrow Dan,' said Max. 'We'll do it tomorrow.'

27
HIDING THE SWORD

With the sword safely stowed under Max's bed, the boys decided, there had been enough excitement for one day, and they spent the evening in silent combat on the Playstation, too anxious about the safety of the sword to leave the room.

The following morning was a beautiful warm and sunny one, and both boys were awake early. Max had slept fitfully, his sleep filled with dreams of soldiers and disaster. Danny of course, had slept like a baby, but was still awake early. Tucked under their respective duvets, they whispered a strategy for the day. The day they had been planning for since that first meeting with Bill way back at the start of the year.

'So Max, let me get this straight in my head. After breakfast, we go down to the cellar, with the sword and a torch. We climb through the hole, under the shelf and follow the tunnel back to the door which connects it to the other tunnel,' Danny sounded confident.

'Exactly that,' said Max 'that is the simple bit. We leave the sword there and come back for the arrowhead.'

'Ok, I've got that. Get the arrowhead, and head around the ring to the hedge, under the hedge to 1861 and meet up with Charlie. I expect they will be wondering whether we found the sword or not. I can't wait to show them Max, and tell them all about it.' Danny pushed back the covers on his bed. 'Let's get on. I don't want to wait any longer.'

The boys were up, dressed, breakfasted and ready for their day within the hour. George had already left for work, so the coast was pretty much clear to collect the sword. As they came down the stairs, with Max in front of Danny, who held the sword under his arm like a rifle, the telephone rang. Martha appeared from Grandpa Sid's room where she had been dusting, and grabbed it.

'Hello,' said Martha quietly. 'Oh hello Gill. Yes, he's fine. Yes, they've been having a wonderful time exploring.' There was a pause while the caller spoke at length. The boys stepped back up the stairs and into the bedroom, closing the door behind them. It was 5 minutes before they heard the phone returned to its cradle. Then Martha called up to them, to come down.

'That was your mum Danny.'

'Oh,' Danny's heart sank. He had been having such a great time staying with the Perry's, he had almost forgotten it was just a two-week holiday.

'She said she has some tickets for a theme park and weekend away, so they will be picking you up a day early.' Martha smiled to Danny. 'We will be sad to see you go, but you can't miss a theme park weekend, far more exciting than our boring park Dan,' she could see a glimmer of disappointment in Danny's eyes. 'You can come back again in the next school holidays, but you will need to pack your things together today.'

'Ok Mrs Perry, I don't have much,' he glanced at Max, 'I can easily do it tonight.'

'That's fine, I'll leave you both to enjoy your last day together. No trouble you hear?' The boys hesitated awkwardly, and smiled until Martha turned back to her cleaning.

With the sword safely back within their grasp, and the coast definitely clear this time, the boys crept out of the back door and around to the cellar. Max unlocked the door and they descended the stone staircase, stopping at the bottom where they collected the torch.

'Right Max, you kneel down and wriggle through the hole, while I shine the torch for you.' Danny was keen to get on, and took the sword and torch. Max wriggled through the boarded-up entrance to the tunnel, with just a sliver of the torch beam for comfort. He had forgotten how cold it was, and a shiver ran through his body.

'Come on Dan, pass me the sword. We need to get on, it's chilly down here.' The sword appeared under the boarding, followed by Danny's outstretched arm holding the torch, as he wriggled through. Both upright, and with the torch held in front, fully lighting up their way, they were able to move quickly down the narrow tunnel single file. The modern torch gave so much more light than the oil lamp they had used previously, and the boys agreed to take it with them back in time, once they had placed the sword safely at the end of the tunnel.

After a few minutes of walking briskly, through webs and negotiating small piles of fallen debris, they reached the door. It was exactly as they remembered, but a secure wooden strut had been placed across it, and nailed in place. It must have been put there when the tunnel entrance had been boarded up in the cellar. This had clearly happened in recent times, to coincide with the boarding up of the tunnel. Max decided it was something else to ask his dad about. History was becoming more appealing the more he discovered. This park seemed to have plenty of it. Max leant the sword up against the wall by the door, then hesitated, before nodding to Danny to turn back and retrace their steps.

With the sword safely in place, the boys retraced their steps home, swiftly negotiating the boarded-up cellar entrance and climbing the steps back out into the sunshine.

'I'll just nip back inside to get the arrowhead,' said Max 'you wait here for me.'
Max was less than a couple of minutes, before re-joining Danny by the garden gate. They took the regular route past the Yew Tree Circle, and the orchard, down into the ring and around to the paddock.

'Max,' Danny paused, grabbing his friend gently by the arm 'this is it. This is going to be my last time travelling adventure of the holiday.' Max smiled.

'Come on then, let's make it a memorable one!' And they ran up the side of the ring ditch as they had done so many times before, and slid under the hedge with ease.

The paddock was horse free, so with a glance around to make sure there were no adults in close proximity, they ran across to the stable. From the corner of his eye, Danny saw movement in an upstairs window. When he looked up, he could see Albert waving frantically, and then he disappeared from view.

'I just saw Albert, at that window,' said Dan, as they made their way to the back door. 'I bet he's on his way down here now he has seen us.'

Sure enough, as they reached the door, and before they could so much as knock, the door opened and there stood Albert, grinning. He pulled Danny in to the kitchen and gave him a brief friendly hug. He seemed very pleased to see them both.

'I've been watching from the landing window since day break. I hoped you'd come back today. Oh no.' Albert's smile changed to a frown. 'You don't have it?' He was clearly referring to the sword.

'Oh yes, I mean no, I mean yes.' Danny confused Albert with his garbled explanation. 'It's like this Albert. We found it. Oh it is amazing. Just the most incredible thing we have ever found. Isn't it Max?' Danny turned to Max who was just behind him in the doorway.

'Let's get in and find Charlie,' said Max 'and then we can explain. Is the cook about?' Max peered over the other boys' shoulders into the empty kitchen. It didn't look like anyone was there.

'No, everyone is out, and Charlie is already down in the cellar sorting out a coal delivery. We can use the kitchen entrance here,' and Albert opened the now familiar kitchen door to the cellar, which they had been bundled through on their first exploratory visit. The three boys descended the steps and found Charlie stacking sacks of coal only a few yards in.

'Charlie!' Danny's exuberance on seeing the servant boy was heart-warming. 'We found it, and now we've come to find Oswulf.'

'Oswulf?' said Charlie and Albert, in exactly the same questioning tone used by Danny and Max a day earlier.

'That's his name. The soldier. Anyway, do you want to know what we found or not?' Danny was in control again. The Victorian boys nodded. They all sat down on the stone steps and Danny gave them a detailed account of the previous day's excitement, and of how they placed the sword at the end of the tunnel, just behind the door, ready to be collected. After the tale had ended, Max stood up.

'So now we need to get the sword, and then the soldier. Albert, you need to lead the way.' Assertively Max gave his command, and they didn't need telling twice.

They knew it was not far down the tunnel, as Max and Danny had found this out the first time. That was when they had taken the fork which lead to a dead end, and a door without a handle. Now they knew of the other door, set back which lead them to Mr Rowbottom's house. Max's house now. So that is where they went first. Max used the bright torch to shine the way. It filled the wider part of the tunnel with light which had Charlie intrigued once again.

'You can have it Charlie. My torch. Once we've sorted out this mystery once and for all. I'll leave the torch with you.' Max really was keen to finish the challenge set. The urgency could be heard in his voice.

It could be a matter of minutes now. A sword to collect and a soldier to deliver. Then home. Could it be that easy?

28
THE FINAL HURDLE

The tunnel may have been brighter, using a modern torch to light the way, but it wasn't any warmer. All four boys shuffled through in silence to the second tunnel entrance, which branched off towards Mr Rowbottom's house, and Albert opened the door. Max's heart was beating faster. He was anxious to find the sword in place, and have it in his hands again. They were so close, he didn't dare to believe it could be this easy.

As Albert opened the door, and shone the beam into the tunnel, there was an initial heart sinking moment. An empty tunnel as far as the beam would shine, lay before them.

'Don't panic, we can't see behind the door from this angle, remember Dan I placed it right at the very end of the tunnel.' Max encouraged Albert, who was in front, to move forward. Albert stepped into the tunnel and felt behind the door.

'I can feel something.' Albert shone the torch back towards his friends, lighting up their faces, and causing them all to shout.

'Put the torch down, Albert, you're blinding us with that light,' Danny was keen to get in and do the retrieving himself, 'now can you just lift it? Carefully now.' Relief flooded through Max as the familiar hessian sack containing the sword, was lifted from the tunnel, and placed in front of the group.

'I think we should leave it in the sack, and go and find Oswulf,' said Max, his anxiety level still high.

'Well I think we should have a look at the sword. Just to be sure you aren't tricking us,' said Albert, with his hand still firmly around the hessian cover.

'You are very quiet Charlie,' said Dan to the smaller boy, 'what do you think we should do?'

'Oh, I don't mind, but do you think we will be long? Molly will be wondering where I am.' Charlie was supposed to be working. It was ok for the other boys, they didn't have the same responsibility as he did.

'Don't worry Charlie, we can get on quickly now.' And turning to the other boys Max repeated his plea for them to take it as it was. Reluctantly they agreed, and backing out of the tunnel completely, they closed the door.

'Right Albert, which way to find Oswulf?' Danny looked to the young Master of the house, who had confessed to the kidnap of their missing soldier. Albert gestured right, moving to the front again.

'It is just up here where this main tunnel forks.' They took the left fork, just as Danny and Max had done on their first visit. The tunnel came to an abrupt dead end, and still there appeared to be no handle on the door. Albert shone the torch down onto the bottom right corner of the door. Barely visible, was a small opening, and Albert leant down pushing his hand into the hole. There was a clunk which released a lock holding the large wooden door closed. It began to open, just enough for Albert to get his hands behind. He pulled hard, and slowly the door opened.

The boys stood in silence, as there at last, before them, on his knees as if in prayer, was their Saxon soldier.

'Oswulf?' Danny whispered to the frightened man. 'It's ok,' his voice was soothing as he reassured the soldier, 'we have come to take you home.'

'I think we should give him his sword,' whispered Charlie. 'He doesn't understand what you're saying Dan. It would be a peace offering.'

'I think Albert should do it,' whispered Danny in reply. 'Albert, you need to show him you are no longer a threat.' Dan was showing his sensible side.

'You are right, let me through.' As Albert slowly stepped forward with the sack cloth in his hand, Oswulf stood up and stepped backwards, still a fearful look in his eyes. 'I will not hurt you. I bring you this.' Albert slowly leant forward and placed the sword, in its bag, on the floor in front of Oswulf. He then knelt down in front of it. The other boys were silent as the sword was slowly unwrapped. Glancing up at the man and nodding to reassure him, Albert drew out the sword from the sack and placed it on the stone floor. He stepped back, as Oswulf, overcome with a mixture of anguish and relief fell to his knees in front of the sword, crying out in his own language, a wail, they assumed, of joy.

'Now how are we going to get him to Bill?' Dan spoke directly to Max. 'That is going to be tricky, when he doesn't understand us. I hope that now he has his sword back, he doesn't think to use it on us!' half joking, Danny gave a forced laugh.

'We need to get him to the Yew Tree Circle. That is where I first met Bill, and where I found the arrowhead. Bill didn't say where exactly, so that is where I think we should go.' While the boys had been talking, Oswulf had stood up tall, and lifting his sword, had slid it back into its scabbard. He was ready to go. He nodded to Max as if to say he understood what was happening. The way out, had to be back through the kitchen and out of the back door. They had to keep everything crossed that no one would be about.

It was easy to coax Oswulf from his prison cell. He stepped out and followed Albert, who walked ahead with Charlie, and the other two boys followed behind. At the cellar steps, Albert turned to whisper instructions. Charlie would go up to check Cook and Molly were distracted, and open the back door for them. Charlie didn't want to go any further.

'I'm going to miss you Charlie,' said Danny, giving Charlie a hug goodbye. 'I have got to go home tomorrow, to some crummy theme park.' Charlie raised his eyebrows and smiled. He hadn't the faintest idea what Danny was talking about.

'We will come back to see you again soon though,' chipped in Max 'and you can come back to my house properly next time, and play with my games, and see my brother and my mum, and..'

'Yeah' interrupted Danny 'and I'll visit Max again, so I'll be there too.' He was eager not to miss out, the adventure really was coming to an end. What this small Victorian boy understood about the two funny friends he had made, was very little, but just having friends and some freedom was everything to him. He shook Max's hand, as they all hovered at the bottom of the staircase.

'Don't you worry about Charlie,' said Albert 'he is my friend now, and I'll make sure he is looked after. I will get him nice clothes, and special treats.' Charlie's grin widened. He had made a proper friend in Master Albert.

'Thank you, Master Albert. I am most grateful for your kindness.' Charlie turned to climb the steps.

'That's no problem, Charlie. And please, no more 'Master Albert'. Call me Bertie from now on.'

'Thank you,' he paused 'Bertie,' and with a positive glow, Charlie climbed the steps to the kitchen.

29
FAREWELL

Oswulf had been locked in a dark, cold cell for several months, and the brightness as he entered the kitchen courtyard in daylight, was almost overwhelming. He held his hand to his eyes, squinting, but keeping the other hand firmly on his sword.

'We can take him from here,' said Max to Albert. This was to Albert's great relief and he didn't argue. It meant his secret, and his ordeal was now over. His parents hadn't discovered the secret, and in a funny way it had had a positive outcome for Albert, although he still felt guilt for what he had done. But he had made three new friends. One of whom lived under his own roof. He was determined to help Charlie now, to live a better life than the one he had known so far. This shared adventure made them firm friends in his eyes.

'Thank you Max. Thank you Danny, for all you have done. It has been fun meeting you. I hope I will see you again soon?' Albert really did hope to meet up again, and like Charlie, he was unaware of the distance these boys had travelled when they had discovered him, Charlie and this grand Manor House. Perhaps if they did meet again, the 21st century boys could try and explain about their magical time travelling adventure. For now, Max and Danny had to say their goodbyes, taking a confused Oswulf with them.

The two boys stood either side of their soldier, guiding him back across the courtyard, to the paddock. He went willingly. As they reached the fence, with sign language and other hand gestures, they communicated with Oswulf, and successfully got him over the fence and across the paddock.

'This bit is going to be tricky Dan,' said Max, when they reached the hedge. 'We aren't all going to be able to go through together, but I think if I go through pulling Oswulf, and you hold on to him from the back, our connection will keep us all travelling through time together.'

'Ooh, listen to you, you time travelling expert,' teased Dan 'but yes, I think we can only try it. You drag him down, and point to the hedge.' They managed in a very untidy, clumsy fashion to get through the small hole they had made before. On the other side, due to the steepness of the hill, Max rolled down, followed by Oswulf. His sword clanking at his side. They ended up in a heap in the well of the ring ditch, spontaneously laughing. It was the first time Oswulf had spoken since his howl of joy at being reunited with his sword. Danny joined them, giving them both a hand to stand upright, and smiled at Oswulf.

'I know you don't understand me, but we are taking you home now.' Oswulf gave a sort of nod as if he understood.

'Right Dan, just a short walk to the Yew Tree circle, and fingers crossed Bill shows up,' with the soldier between them, they walked determinedly around the ring. At the ancient yews, they waited. No sign of Bill, but there was a worrying sound. A vehicle, which sounded like George's big tractor, was heading their way.

'Quick Dan, duck down behind this big beech trunk. I'll drag Oswulf with me to the other pile of cut logs. Wriggle down until he has passed us.' Both boys darted off to hide, with Max dragging an already confused Oswulf with him to a very large pile of recently felled diseased chunks of beech trunk. As the tractor approached, with the sound getting louder Max looked anxiously to Oswulf. This poor confused man. They were so close to finding him the way home. The engine noise trailed away, when a familiar voice came from nowhere.

'Max! Young Max. And Danny of course. Stupendous, marvellous, wonderful, amazing – but not surprising! Well done boys.' Bill was effusive in his praise. Adjectives gushing from this small odd grinning man.

Max and Danny both got up and brushed the dead leaves from their clothes. Oswulf was already standing, facing Bill. He gave the impression he knew who he was, or perhaps why he was there. Oswulf looked relaxed, and no longer had that frightened look in his eyes.

'Boy are we glad to see you,' said Max 'that was close, when dad drove past on his tractor.'

'We have brought you the missing soldier,' said Dan 'and I think we are both ready to go home for a rest now!' Danny grinned 'A rest from time travelling, eh Max?'

'Defo,' said Max 'I feel drained.' Max smiled at Bill and Oswulf. As he did so, Oswulf fumbled in a leather pouch he had beneath his uniform, and holding out his hand, placed a gold coin in

163

each of the boys' hands. Max looked down at his palm, struggling to take it in. A solid gold Saxon coin.

'Wow,' Danny looked across at Max. 'Real treasure.'

'A simple reward, and token of his thanks,' Bill explained 'he really is very grateful to you boys. You have made excellent time travellers, and detectives too. You travelled through time to discover the true Wendlesbiri – the name used by the Romans for the place you now live in. You discovered some of its secrets and uncovered its treasures. Off you go now, back home. You've earned a rest. Oswulf is free and I can now reunite him with his people.' Bill's smile was one of genuine thanks.

While the boys gazed again at their special golden coins, in silence Bill and Oswulf took a step towards the Yew Tree Circle, and were swallowed up in the magic of the Magog woodland.

'He's done it again,' said Max, 'he has simply disappeared.'

'I think there will be more magic to come, in your woodland Max,' said Danny to his best friend 'and do you know what?'

'What?' said Max, now tired and ready for home.

'We are part of that magic now. And no one can ever take that away.' Max nodded.

And with that, the boys linked arms, and turned down the leafy track, for home.

~THE END~

BEVERLEY E GIBBS

26872793R00094

Printed in Poland
by Amazon Fulfillment
Poland Sp. z o.o., Wrocław